THE ALIEN SKILL SERIES

Whistler Independent Book Awards 2022
GOLD MEDAL WINNER
Children's Category

Reader's Favorite Book Awards 2021

GOLD MEDAL WINNER - Category Preteen

Wishing Shelf Book Awards 2019-2020
SILVER MEDAL WINNER
Category Teenagers

Feathered Quill Book Awards 2021
FINALIST - Category Young Readers.
IAN Book of the Year Awards 2020
FINALIST - Category Juvenile.

Reviews:

"The reveals are monumental."

*"The worst thing about the book
is that it ended."*

BEN
ARCHER

and

THE MOON PARADOX

The alien's choice.

Rae Knightly

For information, go to :
www.raeknightly.com

Cover design by PINTADO
Book Formatting by Derek Murphy @Creativindie
Published by PoCo Publishers
ISBN E-Book: 978-1-989605-13-4 / Paperback: 978-1-989605-14-1 / Hardcover: 978-1-989605-15-8

Second Edition: May 2020

For my parents,
Pierre and Nicole.

CONTENTS

CHAPTER 1 *Bob M.*

When Ben and Laura stepped through the elevator door into the penthouse, they found Bob M. waiting.

Not that Ben took much notice: at that point, he felt emotionally and physically drained. He slouched behind his mother, studying the marble floor, anxiously waiting for her to get over the tedious but obligatory introductions, and then, maybe, they would finally let him get some rest.

Hang on for a bit longer.

A movement out of the corner of his eye startled him.

Tike?

But it had only been a flickering shadow cast by candlelight on the countertop of an open kitchen.

Ben swallowed.

He had already caught himself thinking that his dog was scampering at his feet several times in the past days, sending flashes of raw pain through his body. But that wasn't possible, of course.

Tike's dead.

"Laurie, baby!" The man who greeted them as they entered the tenth-floor penthouse, reached out his arms and pecked Laura's left and right cheeks. He stood back and held her by the shoulders so he could take a better look at her. "It's been so long!"

Ben heard the strain in his mother's voice. "Hello, Bob."

He glanced over her shoulder, remembering that Bob was the last name on the list his grandfather had left them, which meant it was someone they could trust.

The man with short, brown hair and neatly trimmed beard stuck his hands in his pockets casually. "Long trip?" he asked, drawing his eyebrows together.

Laura nodded. "Yes, we've been travelling for three days non-stop and just walked from the Greyhound Station."

Bob sighed. "You should have told me. I

would have picked you up."

Laura shrugged. "It's okay. I didn't want to bother you..." She glanced around the apartment. "...and I wouldn't have come if I'd known you were having a party."

Ben realized there were wine glasses on the kitchen countertop and chatting voices coming from a balcony.

To their surprise, Bob burst out laughing. "This? A party? Oh, come on, baby. Have you forgotten already? This is Toronto. It's Friday night. This is just a little get-together." He cleared his throat as if he hadn't meant to laugh so hard. "Don't worry about it. These are just some friends. I'll introduce you to them later. But I guess you want to freshen up first."

Ben stared at his own frumpled clothes and muddy snow boots, suddenly aware of his appearance. After all, Bob wore an elegant, black suit and white shirt, unbuttoned at the neck. He fit perfectly in the minimalist apartment with uninterrupted windows overlooking the Toronto skyline.

"And, who's this?"

Laura had been standing before Ben this whole time, for which he was grateful, but now she moved aside purposefully and placed a hand on his shoulder. "Bob, this is Benjamin. Benjamin, this is Bob."

Ben glanced at his mother. "Bob M.?" he whispered. He hadn't really cared to ask where they were going until then.

She nodded.

"Is he a wit..." He was going to say "witness of *The Cosmic Fall*," but she widened her eyes in warning and cut him off, "This is Bob *Manfield*."

Ben turned his attention from his mother to the man, confused. "Manfield? Isn't that Dad's last name?" His mind whirled.

Bob tilted his head, his brown eyes boring into Ben's. He held out his hand, which Ben accepted. "Hey there, squirt," he said. He glanced briefly at Laura, then added, "I'm your Uncle Bob."

Ben searched his mother's eyes, but she looked away.

Bob shook Ben's hand firmly, and for an instant, the boy forgot about their troubles.

I have an uncle!

"It's good to see you again, Benjamin. It's been too long," Bob said, putting extra stress on the last words. He couldn't take his eyes off Ben and looked as though he were hoping for recognition from the boy.

Laura shifted and placed a hand on Ben's shoulder again. "Actually, everyone just calls him Ben. And we're pretty tired, Bob. Do you think we could talk later?"

"Of course," Bob clapped his hands together, smiling. "Follow me." He led the way into a stylish living room with black sofas and a glass coffee table.

Ben spotted several elegantly dressed people on the balcony which was decorated with white, Christmas-styled lights and candles, while upbeat jazz music played at a decent volume—enough to lighten conversation without drowning it.

A young woman wearing a tight, one-piece dress entered the apartment with a glass of wine in her hand. With the other, she removed her high-heeled sandals and thrust them aside, then smiled when she spotted them. "Hey, Bobby! There you are!" she called, pattering lightly over to them. "Who are your friends?"

"Hi, Pearl," Bob said. "This is Laura Archer. And this is her son, Ben. He's my nephew."

Pearl squealed. "Your nephew? You never told me you had a nephew. Look at him! He's your spitting image. But much more handsome." She squeezed Ben's cheek.

Ben prayed the dimly lit apartment hid his

crimson face.

"This is Pearl," Bob said, seeming a bit jumpy. "She works for me."

Pearl waved a manicured hand at him. "Yeah, right. I clean up after you, honey." She rolled her eyes at Laura. "He has such a scattered brain, this one. You'd think he'd be capable of organizing a simple social event, but guess who did all *this*." She waved a hand at the decorated balcony.

Bob wrapped his arm around her shoulders. "Yes, all right. I couldn't do it without you, baby. You know that."

She smiled approvingly, then waved her wine glass at Laura, "So, is it just you two, then?"

"...and Mesmo," Ben blurted.

Laura tensed sharply beside him.

Bob frowned. "Mesmo? What's a Mesmo?" Then his eyes widened. "Hold on a minute! No cats in my house. I hate cats. I'm allergic."

Picturing Mesmo as a cat, Ben snorted before he could stop himself.

Laura coughed into her hand. "Hum. Mesmo is a friend. And no, he won't be staying. It's just the two of us."

"I see," Bob said, raising an eyebrow. Then, addressing Pearl, he explained, "Laura and Ben arrived from the West Coast earlier. They'll be staying with me for a while."

Pearl's face brightened. "How lovely! I'll finally have a decent girlfriend to talk to." She winked at Laura, then turned to Ben. "And you? Have you ever been to Toronto before?"

"Erm... n-no."

"Really?" she exclaimed. "You'll love it here! There's so much to do. Have you seen the CN Tower?" She took his hand and skipped lightly to the window with him in tow. "Look! You can see it from here."

Ben swallowed and glanced back at his mother who directed a small smile at him.

* * *

Laura woke with a start. She stared at the darkness, trying to remember where she was. She had only meant to lie down for a couple of minutes, but instead, had fallen fast asleep, fully dressed, in the bedroom Bob had provided for her and Ben.

A light tapping on the door made her jump. She realized it was the sound that must have woken her. She rolled over and found Ben sleeping beside her, also fully dressed. He hadn't even taken off his boots.

She stood and quietly opened the door a crack.

"Hi," Pearl whispered. "I didn't want to wake Ben."

Laura nodded, blinking the sleep from her eyes.

"Um, I didn't want to wake you, either, but we ordered sushi and Bobby said you might be hungry. Do you want to join us?"

Laura turned to check that Ben was still sleeping, trying to figure out what to do.

"I made Ben a sandwich, earlier," the young woman said as if reading Laura's mind.

"Thanks," she replied gratefully, not used to having someone take care of things for her. She felt tired, but she was starving, too. Should she step out in her muddy clothes? The idea of mingling with a crowd of well-dressed, casual people was daunting.

"Um," Pearl interrupted her thoughts. "Bobby said you didn't bring any luggage. I thought maybe you'd be more comfortable in this." She held up a black dress.

Now, where did she get that from? Laura wondered.

"Bobby entertains every weekend. I always

keep a spare dress around," Pearl said, seeming to read her every thought.

Laura accepted it, studying the young woman curiously. "Are you and Bob..." she began.

"...together?" Pearl finished. She rolled her eyes. "Oh, goodness, no! We'd get into each other's hair all the time. He's so unpredictable. It drives me crazy."

She's trying too hard, Laura realized.

Pearl locked eyes with her. "What about you? I guess you and Bobby have quite a history?"

Laura dropped her eyes. "Yes. But that was a long time ago..." She let the phrase hang. Then she smiled at Pearl. "Thanks for the dress. We won't be staying long—a couple of days at the most. I'll make sure to return it to you before we leave."

Did a wave of relief pass briefly before the woman's eyes?

Pearl grinned. "Well, go on then. Try it on. We'll be waiting for you." She waved as she turned to leave.

Laura closed the door and let out a long, shaky breath. Her heart pounded in her chest. Had this been a bad idea? Something in the back of her mind told her it was, but she had no choice. Ben worried her more than she cared to admit. The events that had taken place on the Kananaskis

Mountains were excruciatingly fresh in her mind. She needed a place where she could watch over him and make sure he hadn't come out with permanent injuries—physical or mental.

"That goes for me, too," she thought sarcastically, heading for the attached bathroom.

The hot water from the shower triggered a flow of emotions, and she found herself sobbing as she let go of the stress of the past days. She cried for Ben, she cried for Tike, and she cried for Mesmo, who hadn't given a sign of life since their escape from the mountain. She wished she could go back in time and do things differently.

By the time she stepped out of the bedroom wearing the cocktail dress, she had resolved that, from now on, she would do whatever necessary to let things end well.

"Ooh, look at you!" Pearl quipped when Laura stepped onto the balcony. She took Laura's hands and extended her arms so she could see the dress better. "It suits you perfectly." She placed her arm through Laura's own and directed her into the crowd. "Come on, I'll present you."

CHAPTER 2 *An Honest Conversation*

Laura sagged into the living room couch as soon as the last guests entered the elevator. She had put on a false smile and made polite conversation well into the night, thankful that her years working as a server in bars and restaurants had taught her the appropriate social manners to survive through the evening.

"Bye, honey," Pearl said as she kissed Bob on the cheek. The young woman waved at Laura, who returned the gesture. Then the elevator swallowed her up, and Laura was left alone with Bob Manfield.

He removed his dark jacket, threw it to a chair, then settled into the couch opposite her with a plastic water bottle in his hand. He crossed his ankle over his knee and rested his arm on the back of the couch in a relaxed stance. "So," he said after drinking a sip of water. "Here we are."

Laura noticed an unruly mesh of hair sticking out from the back of the man's head, and felt a pang of recognition. She cleared her throat and gestured to the apartment. "Is this yours?" she asked, her mind still in a polite-conversation mode.

Bob nodded with a gleam in his eye. "Yup. It's all mine. I bought it a year ago. I still have unpacked boxes in storage, though. It's been too busy, what with my business expanding and everything..."

Laura wasn't really listening. Facing Bob in flesh and bone after so many years destabilized her. Sure, his brown beard and nice outfit were new, but for the rest, he hadn't changed a bit, which didn't help the pile of unresolved emotions she felt for him.

She realized he had stopped talking and was staring at her, so she said hastily, "You've done well for yourself. I'm happy for you."

"Are you, really?" he replied with a touch of scorn.

I don't need this right now, Laura thought.

Out loud, she said, "Yes, I am. Really."

She rested her elbows on her knees and rubbed her arms. "I'm sorry I called you out of the blue like that. I didn't mean to crash in on you, but things didn't work out the way I had planned."

Bob placed the bottle of water on the table and shrugged. "It's okay," he said. "I already knew you were coming."

Laura stiffened. "You did?" Her voice rose in alarm.

He waved a hand at her. "Calm down, baby. There's nothing to worry about." He locked eyes with her. "Your dad warned me you'd come."

"My dad?"

Bob grinned. "Yeah, I know, right? I'm sure I pulled the same face as you right now." He leaned back on the couch and crossed his knees again.

"He came here about six months ago. He was waiting for me in the lobby." Bob chuckled. "I thought he'd come to give me a good beating, I'll tell you! But no, it turns out your old man wanted to have a chat, face-to-face. I invited him up, and he sat right where you are now. He told me, basically, that you and Ben were going to need help and that I wasn't to ask any questions but that I was to give you any assistance you needed. And boy, did he make it clear that I was to accept." Bob laughed out loud.

Laura burst into tears. She pressed her hands to her face hurriedly. This was the last person she wanted to show weakness to, but the mention of her dad hit her hard. It was as if Bob had pointed out that her dad was sitting right next to her and she hadn't even noticed.

Bob fell silent for a second, then said, "Hey, baby! What's the matter? I didn't mean to..." he broke off, his voice thick.

When she finally felt calm enough to peek through her fingers, he was holding a box of Kleenex in front of her. She plucked a couple of tissues and blew her nose. "I'm not your baby," she said gruffly, trying to recover some dignity.

Bob plopped on the couch with his arms resting on his knees, the box of Kleenex hanging loosely in his hands. "Right. Sure, bab... er..." He sighed and shook his head, then said, "How is the old man, anyway?"

Laura pressed the tissues to her face and hiccupped. "He passed away, not long ago," she managed. "Heart attack."

Bob gasped. "Oh, baby, I'm sorry," he exclaimed. He seemed genuinely crestfallen. "I don't believe it! The old oak, gone? Jeez! No wonder you're so upset." He pushed the box of tissues over the table to her side.

They both stared at it for a long moment.

"Do you want to talk about it?" he asked gently.

Laura shook her head. "No." She spoke in a final tone, then straightened. "We won't be staying long, Bob. We just needed a place to land on our feet, then we'll be off again."

"Now wait a minute. I agreed to take you in. And on your own terms at that. But now that you're here—and that *Ben* is here—you can't go disappearing on me. We have an opportunity here..."

"Stop it, Bob!" Laura snapped. "You promised over the phone you wouldn't go there."

"No, you listen here, little lady." He pointed his index finger at her. "Come now, *Uncle* Bob? Are you *serious?*" He snorted. "Ben looks like a smart kid. How long before he realizes Robert and Bob are not brothers, but one and the same? Jeez', baby, everybody knows Bob is a diminutive for Robert." He slapped his leg. "*Uncle* Bob! How did you come up with such a stupid thing?"

Laura glanced in the direction of the room where Ben was sleeping. "Sh! Okay, okay," she whispered through gritted teeth. "It was a dumb idea. I was desperate. But Ben can't handle the truth right now, Bob. Please, trust me! You promised you'd go along with it."

Bob stared at her in obvious irritation, then said with determination, "I want Ben to know I'm his dad."

Laura bit her lip hard. Her mind scrambled for a reply, but she felt so drained. She couldn't handle another drama.

Bob glared at her, and when she didn't answer, he said, "What? Am I not worthy? Is that what you're thinking?"

Please, not now!

Bob fidgeted in apparent anger. "Come on, say it, then! It's not that hard!"

Laura's exhaustion turned to anger. Didn't he understand that this wasn't the right time, nor the right place? Emotions bubbled inside and threatened to explode.

He leaned forward and stared at her with hard eyes. "Say it!"

"You promised you'd watch over Ben!" she burst out. "You said you'd only be gone for five minutes, but you were out for five hours, drinking with your buddies. What kind of a dad gets into a car without a driver's license, crashes into another car, then runs off in a panic?"

Bob didn't move an inch. He waited to make

sure she was done, then said in a low voice, "Now that wasn't so hard, was it?"

They glared at each other.

A candle died out, leaving a smell of burnt wax.

"Look," Bob said. "I can tell you haven't read a single letter I sent you these past eleven years..."

"Thirteen," she corrected.

Bob raised his eyes. "All right, twelve, thirteen, whatever. The point is, if you'd read any of them, you'd know how often I repeated those very phrases to myself, day in, day out, night after night, going over what I'd done, wishing I'd reacted differently, hating myself every single minute for my stupid reaction.

"But you turned a deaf ear on me. You visited me only once in my five-year jail term, and it was to tell me you gave Ben your dad's surname instead of mine, that you told Ben I'd died in the crash and never to contact you again." His pale face trembled with rage. "And I felt so bad I fell for it and agreed."

He intertwined his fingers, their knuckles going white. "And then, it came to me one day. I was wasting my life away—waiting, hoping, praying—for you to forgive me. But I realized, the only one who could forgive me was *me*. If I were ever to move forward, I would need to make my own peace, stop looking back and live my life. I figured no-one was badly hurt in the crash. I paid my dues. So I forgave myself, respected your wish and moved on."

He waved his arms at the apartment. "You could have been part of it, you know? But you chose not to. And I wonder, sometimes, when are *you* going to get over it, Laura?"

His eyes dug into hers, forcing her to look down.

In her haste to find a safe place to hide, Laura had conveniently discarded the thought that this conversation would take place. How wrong she'd been! Had she really thought Bob would let them stay with him without attempting to resolve their decades-old fight?

If it hadn't been for Ryan Archer's contact list, Laura realized she would never have ended up here. *Dad, why did you leave me Bob's number?*

But it was too late now. The day she had always dreaded loomed before her.

Ben is going to hate me.

Bob's stance softened a little. "If you think I no longer care about what I did, you're sorely mistaken. I still think about that crash every day. I was irresponsible and young, I know that. But I'm a grown man now, I've learned from my mistakes. I would never turn my back on you or Ben like that again. You've got to believe me."

Laura studied his face and saw honesty reflected in it. She had shut him away from her life the minute she had learned he had been responsible for the crash, disgusted by his narrow-minded escape after his botched hit-and-run.

We were so young!

They had met in high school. They had been carefree. And then Ben had come along...

She stood and brushed at the folds in her dress. "I don't know if I can ever forgive you, Bob, but that's my problem, not Ben's. It would be selfish of me to continue keeping him from his dad." She took a deep breath. "So, I agree. We'll tell him, together. But please, Bob, give me a week, two at the most. There's something I need to take care of, first."

I have to save Mesmo.

* * *

Ben woke, feeling rested for the first time in a long while. He had had a deep, dreamless slumber, no Tike or Bordock to torment him. He stretched, then realized his mother lay fast asleep next to him. He got out of bed as silently as possible, then took a long, refreshing shower. After days spent on the freezing Kananaskis Mountains and travelling day and night across the country, the hot water felt glorious.

Having to wear his same clothes satisfied him much less, however, but, with no other option, he stepped into Bob's living room with his torn jeans and dirty hooded sweater.

He blinked at the bright light coming in from the windows and ruffled his wet hair, before realizing Bob was sitting on a stool at the edge of the kitchen counter, working on his computer while sipping on a cup of coffee.

"'Morning, squirt," Bob said, turning to face him. "Did you sleep well?"

Ben noticed his uncle's hair was as disheveled as his own, which was a bit of a relief. He smiled and replied, "Hi, Uncle Bob. Yes, thanks."

"I think your mom's going to be knocked out for a good while yet. She went to bed pretty late. We had a lot of catching up to do."

Ben felt a pang of envy at having been left out of the conversation. He would have liked to learn everything he could about his newly-discovered uncle.

"You must be hungry," Bob said, getting off the high stool and opening the fridge. "Ah, you'll have to forgive my manners. This is a typical bachelor's fridge. Not even an old piece of cheese in sight." He straightened and pursed his lips. "How about we get a decent plate of eggs and bacon? I know just the right place!"

Ben wanted to hug the man. "Yes, thanks."

"Okey-dokey. Get cleaned up, and we'll head right out."

Ben's face drooped.

Do I look that messy?

Bob put his hands to his hips. "You don't have anything else to wear, do you?" he said with half a frown.

Ben blushed and shook his head.

"All righty! Looks like we'll be doing some shopping as well, then!" He clapped his hands together.

Ben's nose curled automatically, making Bob laugh. "Oh, come on!" he said, wrapping an arm around Ben's shoulders and directing him towards the private penthouse elevator. "It will be fun! Just you and me. Men only."

Ben grinned. "Thanks, Uncle Bob. I'd like that."

CHAPTER 3 *Beetrix*

Over a hearty breakfast, Bob chatted about life in Toronto. He told Ben how he successfully launched and ran three nightclubs and that he was a big fan of professional ice hockey. He promised he'd take Ben to a game.

But Ben wanted to know about his dad.

Bob shrugged. "Sorry, squirt. I can't say much. I left home pretty young and backpacked around the world for several years. Then, I figured I needed to settle down someplace—do something with my life—and Toronto seemed as good a place as any."

His eyes became distant. "Your dad and I weren't that close. I'm sorry to say he was a pretty irresponsible guy and probably would have continued down that road if things hadn't ended the way they did."

He leaned his arms on the table and bent forward to be eye-level with Ben, who was sipping on his milkshake. "Now, I will tell you this: he and I, we had the magic touch when it came to hockey passes. You should have seen him on the ice! He was the best! A natural skater with loads of potential."

Ben's eyes widened as he imagined his dad sliding on an ice-skating rink, dressed in hockey sportswear. "Really?"

Bob pulled back and grinned. "Yes, really!" He knocked with his knuckles on the table as if to indicate that their conversation had ended and searched for a waitress to pay the bill.

Ben continued to daydream as they left the restaurant and crossed the street to a triangular-shaped park.

"What about you?" Bob interrupted his thoughts.

"Huh?"

"Yeah, what about you, squirt? You haven't told me anything. What types of things do you like?"

Ben swallowed. "Um, I like dogs, I guess."

"Dogs?" Bob said with a touch of

amusement. "Ah, well. These are the types of dogs that I like." He stopped walking, and Ben bumped into him.

They were standing in front of an impressive, two-tiered fountain. Spouts ejected water from the base up, the majority of these originating from a dozen statues placed around the fountain.

In a different life and a different time, Ben would have found these statues amusing, but not so at this very moment, because the figures happened to represent dogs of all kinds. Some were placed outside the fountain, others, inside, and out of their snouts, water arched in clean lines into the basins above.

"We're in Berczy Park," Bob explained. "And this is—you'll never guess—Dog Fountain." He chuckled. "I thought you might like it."

Ben knew he was waiting for some kind of sign of approval, as any typical boy would have, but he couldn't do it. He offered Bob a forced smile. "Cool," he said, struggling to contain his loss. "Can we go, now?" He needed to get away or he was going to break apart.

Bob pouted his lower lip and shrugged. "Sure."

They walked towards busier streets and

glanced absentmindedly at store windows.

"So," Bob said with his hands in his pockets. "Who's this Mesmo guy, anyway? Your mom's boyfriend?"

Ben poofed, then bit his lower lip to get a hold of himself. "No." He giggled, then thought the better of it. "He's a good friend, though. We're supposed to meet him here."

He shut his mouth, wondering if he was saying too much, then suddenly remembered Kimi's surprised face when she had found out that her mother, Maggie, and their host, Thomas, had revealed that they had feelings for each other. Was he missing something similar between Mom and Mesmo?

Adults can be weird in that way.

His thoughts were interrupted when Bob led him into a clothing store and began fishing out jeans, shorts and sweaters. Before long, Bob shooed him into the dressing rooms, his arms laden with clothes. It took Ben a while to sift through the mound.

"Are you okay in there?" Bob called after a long while.

"Humph, I think this shirt is too small." Ben pulled open the curtain to show him.

Bob checked the price tag for the size, then

clicked his fingers. "Off with it. I'll get you a bigger size."

Ben pulled the shirt over his head, then winced. He stared at his chest and found the black mark near his heart—a painful reminder of where Tike had been hit. He removed the shirt with more care and handed it to Bob, but found the man staring at him with deep worry lines on his forehead.

He saw the wound!

"Um... skiing accident in Alberta," Ben muttered.

"Ah," Bob said as he accepted the shirt. "That looks bad. Maybe we should have it checked..."

"Oh no, that's fine." Ben jumped in a little too quickly. "I'm much better already." He closed the curtain in a hurry and shut his eyes to prevent tears.

From then on, the mood between them changed, and even though Bob bought him a cupboard-full of clothing and sneakers, Ben couldn't quite get that frown off his uncle's face for the rest of the morning.

"Do you want to get some ice cream at the lake?" Uncle Bob asked after they were done shopping. It was almost noon.

Ben wanted to go home, but at the same

time he didn't want to darken his uncle's mood further, so he accepted.

They ended up at the edge of a lush park called Tommy Thompson Park, which formed a curious web-like net of paths straight into Lake Ontario. The Canadian/US border ran through the middle of it. Ben squinted, hoping to spot the other side of the vast body of water, but the US shore was too far away.

He sat and rested his back against the trunk of a tree while Bob went to get their ice creams from a local vendor. He stroked the grass with the palm of his hands and enjoyed the occasional ray of the sun on his face.

I wonder if Kimi is eating ice cream, too?

"There's an ice cream truck that sells the best bubblegum flavour in the world. You'll see." Her voice echoed in his head, and he wished he could have stayed in Canmore long enough to taste it.

If you crush me, I'll sting you!

Ben gasped. He looked down and found his hands glowing. Blood rushed to his ears as his alien skill kicked in. He glanced around to make sure no-one had noticed, then stuffed his hands hurriedly in the pockets of his new, hooded sweatshirt.

A gentle humming reached his ears, and

when he searched through the grass with his eyes, he found a rather large bee lumbering around the green stems, close to where his hand had been.

Oops! Sorry!

It seemed proper to apologize. Remembering what Mesmo had taught him, Ben presented himself.

I am Benjamin Archer. May I speak with you?

There was no immediate answer, but rather, a wave of desolation brushed at his mind. Ben quickly set up a mental barrier between his and the bee's feelings.

Hello, Benjamin Archer. I am Beetrix. Yes, we may talk.

Ben smiled briefly at the bee's name, but at the same time knew instinctively that something was wrong.

What's the matter?

The insect brushed at its antennas.

I can't find my hive. My children won't make it without me.

Ben frowned.

Why?

Beetrix buzzed her wings.

Because I am their queen.

Ben's mouth dropped.

No wonder she seems bigger than an ordinary bee.

The thought escaped before he could hold it back, but she heard him anyway. She did not seem to mind, however.

I am larger than the others because I am the mother of a thousand children. They are lost without me—if we are not lost already...

What do you mean?

An illness has spread in our midst. I cannot identify it. I had hoped that, by moving my hive, we would find a healthier home. But that is when we got sepa... aah!"

A gigantic foot stepped on Beetrix, rendering everything dark in Ben's mind.

Bob stood right beside him, plastering the grass with his shoe.

"Get off!" Ben cried, jumping to his feet and shoving his uncle aside.

An ice cream cone slipped out of Bob's hand, its contents splattering to the ground. "Whoa!" he yelled. "Take it easy, squirt!" He gestured toward the grass. "Those things sting!"

"No!" Ben said vehemently. "Not this one." He crouched and searched the grass with his mind.

Beetrix?

A tiny movement indicated she was still alive.

Ben let out a breath of relief.

Beetrix buzzed angrily a couple of times and climbed to the top of a grass stem.

Are you hurt?

She tested her wings.

I am fine. But tell that giant troll to watch where he puts his paws!

Ben fought a smile.

Come with me. I'll help you find your hive.

Beetrix considered the offer for a second, then clambered onto Ben's sleeve and nestled in the boy's hoody.

When Ben stood again, Bob was staring at him with his nose curled and one eyebrow raised. "Are you serious?" he said, licking at his ice cream.

Ben grinned. "Yep." He checked that his hands weren't glowing too much, then picked up the shopping bags with his new clothes inside.

"I'm allergic," Bob warned as they headed out of the park.

"It's okay. I'll tell her not to sting you."

Bob paused a fraction of a second, before biting into the sweet dessert. "You're a weird kid," he said.

"I know."

"And I'm not getting you another ice cream," he added, a drop of white vanilla landing on his beard as he bit into the cone. "This is mine."

Ben laughed. "That's okay. Sugar is bad for kids my age anyway."

They walked, side by side, the dark mood between them having lifted somewhat.

"Uncle Bob?"

"Hm?"

"You know bees like ice cream, don't you?"

CHAPTER 4 *Suspicion*

"Hi, Mom!"

Laura heard Ben greet her as she stepped out of the bedroom. But he didn't stop to talk to her. He dropped shopping bags on the floor and headed straight for the balcony.

She pulled on a sweater and followed him. "Hi, honey. Where have you been?" She wanted to give him a hug, but he said, "Careful!" She pulled back and watched him remove a bee from his hoody with extreme care. His hands glowed a soft, blue colour. He placed the bee on a decorative shrub, then spoke to it, "I'll get you something more comfortable in a bit."

Only then did he turn his attention to Laura. "Her name's Beetrix. She lost her hive. I'm going to help her find it."

Laura smiled and ruffled his hair.

"Oh! And Uncle Bob took me shopping. He bought me tons of clothes and these sneakers." He pointed at the clean, new shoes on his feet.

"Really?" Laura said thoughtfully. "That's nice of him."

Ben nodded, checking up on his new insect friend. "Yeah. He took me for breakfast and everything!"

Laura stopped stroking his hair and stared at him, but he seemed to be in a genuinely good mood.

She let out an inward sigh of relief.

Bob didn't tell him.

"Ben," she said. "Have you heard from Mesmo?"

Her son's face darkened as he shook his head. "I tried contacting him this morning," he said, tapping his wristwatch.

Laura admired the tiny stone in the centre of the watch. It sparkled too much for it to be a diamond, reminding her that it was in fact an alien device used by Mesmo to spirit travel.

Only, Mesmo was not connecting with them.

Laura's heart thumped loudly, but she didn't want Ben to notice her worry. He had enough on his mind. Her thoughts had been on the alien ever since she had seen him last, standing on a snowy ledge, his spirit almost transparent from the effort of having saved them repeatedly on the Kananaskis Mountains. That had been four days ago.

Way too long.

"Keep trying, okay?" she said.

Ben nodded. They both automatically glanced inside the apartment, where Bob was busying himself unpacking Ben's clothes.

"I'm going to stay here for a bit," Ben said, indicating his glowing hands.

"And I'm going to look for a job," Laura said. "Will you be okay on your own?"

He nodded, and they gave each other a quick hug.

Laura stepped back into the living room to find Bob staring at her, as he drank from a bottle of water. He had an unreadable look on his face.

She forced a smile. "Ben said you took him shopping?" She went through the clothing that lay on the edge of the couch. "Thank you," she added, not sure yet if she approved. Hadn't she always been Ben's provider?

He nodded briefly.

Laura tried to fill the silence between them.

"I'll pay you back as soon as I can. I'm on my way to look for a job. Do you mind if Ben stays here in the meantime?"

He took her gently by the wrist, still with that serious look on his face. "Come," he said. "We need to talk." He led her to the kitchen counter and invited her to sit on the high stools.

What now?

"Look, baby," he began. "Why do you need to look for a job? I told you already, I run three successful nightclubs. I'm opening a fourth location in three months. I'm always looking for people..."

She lifted her hand firmly. "I'm not working night shifts again, Bob."

He cocked his head. "Who said anything about night shifts? Hear me out, for once! My accountant is going on maternity leave next month. I need someone I can trust to replace her. She could teach you. It's a nine-to-five job, five days a week. The wage is above average. I treat my staff well, believe it or not."

Laura listened to him with a slight frown. He was speaking with a stern voice that was new to her.

Must be his business voice.

She found herself liking this grown-up side

to him. She couldn't help seeing Ben's face in his, only it was the adult version of the one she'd fallen for so many years ago.

"And there's another thing," he continued, pulling her back into the conversation. "I may not know much about kids, I'll give you that, but I know this boy should be in school right now. There's a private school not far from here. Very well rated. I know the Principal. I could get him registered in a heartbeat." He kept talking, but unexpected feelings washed over her again.

I fend for Ben!

She struggled to push back the emotion.

In less than five minutes, Bob had solved two of her biggest issues: money and keeping Ben occupied. She didn't like it, something in the back of her mind resisted for no sound reason.

Don't be so selfish! It's only until I find Mesmo.

She waited patiently for Bob to finish talking, then said, "All right, I accept. Thank you, Bob."

He gaped, his hand still raised before him as if he was preparing for another round of convincing. "Oh," he said, leaning back. "It's that bad, then?"

She frowned. "What do you mean?"

He sighed and stroked his beard. "The Laura I knew wouldn't have accepted that easily."

She lowered her head. "I guess we all have to grow up sometime." She cleared her throat and stood. "I still need to get some clothes. Don't worry, I'll pay for them myself," she added quickly.

He grabbed her wrist again and bore his eyes into hers. "I don't know what's going on with you two, but I'm not blind." He glanced at her wrist, which still had the mark of Bordock's handcuff on it. "I won't accept anyone hurting you or Ben. Your dad said not to ask questions, but I hope you'll smarten up and spill the beans." He let her go and sat back. "When you feel up to it, that is."

His eyes were glued to her, making it extremely hard for her to maintain her composure. She took a few steps back and nodded unsteadily. "Yes. When I'm ready." She turned before he could say anything else and entered the elevator, letting out a shaky breath as she did so.

* * *

Inspector James Hao stared fixedly at an invisible point on the opposite side of the room. The concrete wall of the Dugout infirmary was dull, to say the least, but after its hasty construction, painting the walls a clean or cheerful colour hadn't exactly been on anyone's mind.

He pouted in concentration, oblivious to his surroundings or the throbbing pain of his broken leg, which lay tightly wrapped in a cast before him on the hospital bed.

Doctors and nurses slid by his open door, going about their business, which suited him fine because right now he was burning with anger. He had placed a lid on his feelings, concentrating solely on getting better so he could get back to work as soon as possible.

A shadow stopped before the crackled glass of the window that separated his room from the corridor. Then a man stepped into the doorframe and leaned against it nonchalantly.

"Hi, partner," Connelly said with his hands in his pockets. "I thought I'd check up on you."

Hao set his jaw, the lid on his inner cauldron sliding off to reveal burning coals.

Connelly entered, checking the room with vague interest. He stopped by Hao's bed and tapped the cast lightly with his fingers. "That looks painful," he said. "Did they tell you how long you'll be in here for?"

Hao signalled for Connelly to approach,

which he did. Then, with lightning speed, Hao grabbed him by the collar and pulled him close, so their faces were inches apart. "You saw me!" he growled. "You saw me, buried in the snow under your feet. And *you left me there*!" Every word was laden with fury and disbelief.

Connelly struggled to release himself from Hao's grip. He pushed against Hao's shoulders, but Hao wasn't going to let him go so easily. Connelly's hands slid closer to his throat.

"Hey! What's going on here?" A woman's voice shrieked down the corridor, "I need assistance!"

There were thudding feet, then several hands tried to unlock the two fighting men from each other. Arms appeared around Connelly's chest, and a doctor yanked him away.

"You saw me!" Hao screamed, his face livid.

Connelly staggered back, then caught himself. In a defiant gesture, he straightened his tie, shot a deathly look at Hao, then stepped out of the room.

"I'm on to you!" Hao yelled after him.

CHAPTER 5 *Headquarters*

The sun reflected so brightly on the skyscraper that Laura had to look away. She stood at the corner of a busy crossing, lost in a crowd of hasty pedestrians who brushed passed her, handbags swaying, work shoes clicking hurriedly on the walkway.

The Victory Air headquarters filled the shiny, window-clad building, with a long set of stairs leading to a modern reception. Some employees sat on the steps, enjoying a ray of sunlight while on their lunch break, or scanning their phones while they chatted with a colleague.

Laura unzipped the raincoat she had bought and straightened her new, olive-green sweater. It had felt good to get rid of the clothing damaged by the frigid weather on the Kananaskis Mountains.

She plunged into a coffee shop opposite the building and lined up for a coffee and sandwich.

"Busy, isn't it?" she said pleasantly to the young man on the other side of the counter who was preparing the items.

"Actually, this isn't too bad," the man said, working the coffee machine. "You should've seen the line-up an hour ago!"

Laura smiled at him. "Is that when all the Victory Air employees have lunch, then?"

The man laughed. "Yeah, I guess so."

"I saw the news yesterday. I thought they were on strike?"

"Yesterday, yes. Tomorrow, who knows? Everybody's expecting the company to announce bankruptcy."

"That's awful," Laura sympathized.

The man shrugged as he passed her her sandwich and punched in the cash amount of the food. "Nah, I wouldn't worry about it. You should see the CEO. He walks up those stairs with his chest puffed, like he owns the world. I bet he's got it all figured out."

Laura stopped counting the coins she had pulled out. "You mean Victor Hayward?" She slid the money towards him slowly.

The man nodded. "He's like a well-oiled clock. You'll see his limo drop him off at 8.45am and pick him up at 6pm sharp, every day. With everything going on, you'd think he'd take a back entrance. But not Victor Hayward. He barges through the crowds of protesters and media as if he didn't have a care in the world."

Laura stepped aside while he spoke as impatient customers made it clear she was taking up too much time. She thanked the man behind the counter and squeezed into a chair facing the window, beside two men working on their laptops.

She stared at the infamous building. Would she find answers here? Would Victory Air or its boss lead her to Mesmo?

She settled in her chair, and waited.

* * *

Hao munched on his lip, then realized he was staring at the wall with a deep frown again. It wouldn't do to lie around for days doing nothing. It was time for some action.

He picked up the phone on his bed stand and pressed an extension.

"Yes, sir?" his assistant said on the other end.

50

"Bring me my laptop. I want access to *The Cosmic Fall* files. Make sure I still have clearance. Also, bring me the boxes in my office. And be quick about it!"

"Yes, sir," the assistant said, but Hao heard the hesitation in his voice. "Hum, but will the High Inspector agr...?"

"Just bring me the damn things and let me deal with the High Inspector."

In his mind's eye, Hao imagined the assistant jump to a salute. "Yes, Sir!"

* * *

Laura fidgeted on her seat. She had been at the coffee shop for almost five hours, and her back hurt. She'd had to spend her last coins on a lemonade when she noticed the baristas at the counter glancing her way.

It was close to five minutes before six when a sleek, black limousine pulled up in front of Victory Air.

Laura pushed back the stool, making it screech on the floor, but she took no notice and was out in a jiffy. She had to wait at the pedestrian crossing until the light turned green, because heavy evening traffic blocked the way, and by the time she made it across the street, the man she had been waiting for was already exiting the building.

She jogged diagonally up the imposing stairs, bumping heavily into one of Victor Hayward's bodyguards. Her handbag flew to the ground.

"Hey, lady! Watch it!" the bodyguard warned, shielding Victor Hayward with his muscled body. He did not need to speak loudly as his stiff posture was indicative enough that he wasn't up for any nonsense.

"I'm so sorry!" Laura apologized. "I wasn't paying attention."

The bodyguard regarded her sternly, then picked up her handbag, giving her a good view of the short man with mixed black-and-grey hair and black-rimmed glasses who was about to enter the limo.

"Mr. Hayward!" she called.

The bodyguard jumped to attention, holding out his hand defensively. "That's enough! Stand back please."

Laura tried to glance behind his hulky body. "Mr. Hayward! It's Laura Archer," she shouted. "From Chilliwack."

Victor Hayward froze with his head already

inside the car. Then he straightened and turned to see who had spoken.

Laura waved and smiled at him, trying to look as innocent and harmless as possible.

The man's suspicious eyes softened. He gestured at his bodyguard to let her pass.

"Mr. Hayward!" she said breathlessly. "Do you recognize me? I'm Ryan Archer's daughter, Laura. You know? Your neighbour in Chilliwack?" She stood before him and held out her hand. "Imagine bumping into you here!"

The CEO of Victory Air shook her hand, then recognition filled his eyes. He broke into a genuine enough smile and said, "Laura? My, my! Yes, I remember you, though if my memory serves me well, the last time we spoke you were about this high..." he lifted his hand parallel to the ground to indicate her height, "...and you were trespassing on my property, if I recall."

Laura let out a giggle, her blush coming out naturally. "Oh, gosh! Please don't remind me. Dad was so angry with me!"

"You can say that again," Hayward said, his grin widening to show a set of small, extra-white teeth. "Ryan came over and apologized profusely. So how is my old neighbour?"

Laura's face fell instantly. "My dad passed

away some months ago, Mr. Hayward. He suffered a major heart attack."

Hayward's grin faded. "Ah, dear girl. I'm sorry to hear that." He glanced around hastily. "Look, I can't talk now. But I want to see you in my office next Monday, 9am sharp. Ask for my Executive Assistant, Charlene. She'll be informed." He slipped into his car and pointed his index finger at her. "Don't be late!"

His chauffeur closed the door on him and hurried to the driver's side.

Laura blew her hair out of her eyes and watched the limo disappear into traffic.

* * *

"Where were you?" Ben asked, standing hastily from the sofa and dropping the X-box control on the coffee table. He'd been out for hours, unsuccessfully looking for Beetrix's hive, and had been disappointed not to find his mother on his return.

Laura removed her raincoat and checked the apartment. "Are we alone?"

Ben nodded. "Uncle Bob's at work. What happened?"

She placed her hand on his shoulder and led

him back to the couch. They sat down and faced each other.

"I saw Victor Hayward," she said, a little out of breath. "I'm meeting him on Monday morning."

"*What?* Are you crazy? How did you do that?"

"He was my neighbour growing up, remember? I know him personally, though not very well, of course. He was away most of the time, but he'd drop by to catch up on local news with Grampa."

Ben shivered. "Do you think he witnessed *The Cosmic Fall?*"

Laura pursed her lips, then nodded. "Yes. I'd bet my bottom dollar on it."

Ben's hands flew to his face. "So now what, Mom? You can't just walk up to him and say, 'hand over the alien.'"

"I know, I know. We have to come up with something."

They both fell silent, deep in thought.

Suddenly Ben's face lit up. "I have an idea."

CHAPTER 6 *A Dangerous Device*

Laura's footsteps echoed on the perfectly polished marble floor. The imposing symbol of Victory Air hung above the impeccable reception where receptionists wearing bandanas with the red-and-grey colours of the company spoke into extra-thin headsets.

One of them glanced up and said, "Good morning, may I help you?"

Laura tried to make herself look important. "Yes, I'm here to see Mr. Victor Hayward."

A brief shadow of disbelief passed before the receptionist's eyes, so Laura added quickly, "My name is Laura Archer. Please refer to his Executive Assistant, Charlene."

The receptionist's fingers were already

typing away and before long, Laura was given a printed badge that allowed her to override the elevator security to reach the CEO office on the top floor.

Laura's legs felt like jelly as she scanned the badge and pressed the highest number on the button panel, a staggering flood of doubt almost making her turn back.

This isn't going to work!

She had argued extensively with Ben, telling him that his idea was way too risky. They could lose contact with Mesmo forever. Not only that, Ben was basing his idea purely on a hypothesis, one they had never tested.

The problem was, they hadn't been able to come up with any other plan. Most of their ideas involved tedious research and time-consuming spying on Victor Hayward. And time was not on their side. Laura was constantly reminded of Mesmo's words: if he did not reach Saturn's moon, Enceladus, within a week, he would never be able to return to his home planet.

She wished they had been able to make contact with the alien to confirm their theory and give him a heads up. But after multiple attempts, Mesmo still had not answered Ben's calls, meaning he was not in good shape.

Or maybe worse.

Laura shuddered.

Hang in there, Mesmo.

She set her jaw, straightened her shirt neck and pulled back a strand of ash blonde hair behind her ear as she watched the floor numbers flash by.

The elevator door pinged and slid open, revealing a posh reception decorated in tones of soft grey and splashes of red.

A woman with shallow cheeks, glasses and a tight bun stood as soon as Laura entered the spacious area from which she caught stunning views of the city.

"Ms. Archer, I presume?" the woman said in a business-like tone, which she had clearly practiced over many years.

"Yes."

"I'm Charlene. Please, follow me." The woman reminded her of a stern middle-grade school teacher.

Laura pinched her lips. In a matter of seconds, she was led into a large office with an impressive oak desk and two leather sofas with an oak coffee table in the middle. Victor Hayward sat in one of these chairs with his legs crossed as he studied documents over his black-rimmed glasses.

He dropped the documents as she

approached and stood to shake Laura's hand. Laura felt his thick, golden ring under her fingers. "Laura," he stated. "Welcome. Can I get you something to drink? Coffee? Tea?"

"Oh, um, a glass of water, please."

Hayward nodded to Charlene, who left instantly, while he invited Laura to sit.

"Thank you for being so timely," he began. "I can't stand people who are late. It's a habit I caught from my line of work. No-one likes a delayed flight, you will agree." He sat opposite her and Laura thanked the stars she had categorically refused to let Ben accompany her.

"It's the least I could do, Mr. Hayward," Laura replied. "I'm surprised you were able to make time for me at all. I appreciate it."

"Nothing's too much for my dearly departed neighbour. I miss him sorely."

Laura glanced at the businessman, trying to determine whether he was being genuine, but Hayward showed nothing of his feelings. She shuddered at the thought that he could be holding Mesmo against his will.

"So, tell me, what brings you to the city?"

Laura accepted a glass of water from Charlene and said, "I needed a change of setting. You know, to get away from the memories..."

"Yes, of course. Both of your parents passed away, if I remember correctly. There isn't much holding you back on the West Coast, is there?"

Laura shook her head, going along with the small talk, wondering what she should say next.

"And... what is your line of work, exactly?"

Laura's throat went dry, so she took a sip of water. "Oh, uh, I wasn't much good in school. I didn't get a degree or anything like that. I've been working odd jobs here and there."

And taking care of Ben.

"I see. Well, if there's anything I can do in that department, don't hesitate. Charlene can set you up with Human Resources and look at your options..."

"Oh, no, no. There's no need. I've already found a job. But, thank you."

Hayward rubbed at his chin, then narrowed his small, green eyes. "Don't let the media get to you, Laura. They are pure sensationalists, shouting to all who will hear that Victory Air is taking a dive. But they have no idea what I have in store for them. My company is at the dawn of its existence, not at its end."

He stood and paced before the windows overlooking Toronto and Laura could hear the pride in his voice. "The media is not far from the truth, Laura. Oil is a thing of the past. It's time to fuel our cars and planes with brand new, cutting-edge technology."

His hand curled into a fist, as if he were holding a miniature Earth within it. "Victory Air holds that technology, the power to generate unlimited, low-cost energy for all!"

Laura felt the blood drain from her face.

So that's what he's after!

She understood everything now, Victor Hayward needed the alien to reveal the source of energy that fueled his spaceship. Hayward would use it for his own airplane company. Investors, governments, the military... all would flock to him to get their hands on such a source of power.

She almost dropped her glass of water as she placed it on the edge of the table. She was no longer able to concentrate on the magnate's self-centered speech, but nodded in what she considered were appropriate places.

Hayward sat heavily in the sofa, the leather squeaking under his weight. "But enough of that. This is our little secret, between you and me, and is a work in progress." He tapped the tips of his fingers together and bore his eyes into hers.

She braced herself as she sensed more was coming, then picked up the glass again to keep her nervous hands busy.

"Tell me about *The Cosmic Fall*," he said.

Laura lurched, spilling some water. "The... the what?"

He leaned back as if he were suddenly tired. *"The Cosmic Fall.* You've heard of it, of course. Did you know it occurred on my land?"

"It... it did?"

"Yes. Picture this: some interstellar rocks lurch towards the Earth and, bingo! they fall right into my lap, so to speak. You'd think anything that landed on your property belonged to you, but no, the government stepped in and took it all away from me. I was wondering, did that happen to your father, too?"

What's he getting at?

"Er... no, of course not..." she stammered.

He nodded, raising his eyes to the ceiling as if in deep thought. "I didn't think so. However, considering your precarious financial situation, I am sure you will be happy to hear that I am interested in purchasing your father's house and land, since you clearly have no further use for it. How would you like to step out of my office with a two million dollar check in your pocket?"

Laura's jaw dropped.

She made a superhuman effort to close her

mouth and swallow a large lump in her throat. "Th-that's unexpected. I... um... would need to think about it."

He waved his hand at her. "Of course! Of course! It's a lot to take in. But my offer is on the table. You should take it while the deal is hot because I can't promise it will still be there tomorrow."

"Thank you." Laura forced the words out. She was on the verge of a nervous breakdown.

I need to finish this!

She stood hastily, as did he.

"Here's my card," he said. "Call me anytime. I'll even add in an extra two hundred grand, as a last show of goodwill to my dear neighbour."

She took the card hastily. "Thank you, Mr. Hayward. You're very kind. I will consider your offer." She needed to change the subject at once, or she would crumble.

It's now or never!

She opened her handbag and said, "Talking about goodwill, I have something for you, as well."

She pulled out a square box, neatly wrapped in grey paper with a red ribbon around it. "It's not as generous as your offer, of course, but I wanted you to have this."

Hayward glanced at her in surprise, then

proceeded to remove the wrapping. A velvet box appeared, resembling one that would contain a wedding ring. Only, this one was bigger.

"What's this?" Hayward said, opening the lid.

"It was my father's," Laura explained. "I have no use for it. It's a men's model. I think Dad would have felt very honoured to have Victor Hayward wear it."

The businessman pulled out a silver watch and studied it closely.

"You see?" Laura said, pointing to its centre. "It even has a diamond in it. Go on. I want to see it on your wrist."

* * *

Inspector Hao burst into High Inspector George Tremblay's office, located at level -1 of the Dugout, ignoring the assistant who tried to stop him.

"Why does Victor Hayward have access to the spaceship?" he blurted.

Documents slid out of his hands as he tried to keep a hold on his crutches. He swore, then bent with his cast leg teetering dangerously in the air, until he managed to recover the papers.

When he straightened again, the High

Inspector—who cast a distasteful look his way—said into his phone, "I'll call you back." He hung up, then waved the assistant away.

Hao hopped inside the office and landed in the chair opposite his boss.

"James," the High Inspector greeted, his voice absent of emotion. "I see you're up and about."

Hao dropped the documents on the desk and stabbed his finger at them. "Why does a civilian witness to *The Cosmic Fall* have access to the spaceship?" he repeated, ignoring the greeting.

The High Inspector remained impassive. "Agent Connelly is a civilian witness, as well," he noted. "And he has access to the spaceship."

"Yes. But this is different. Why wasn't I notified? Why did I have to go through the registry to find out?"

"Victor Hayward isn't just anybody. After making his witness deposition, he offered us his own flight engineers—some of the best in the country. His navigational expertise can help us pierce the mysteries of the extraterrestrial spacecraft. Not to mention that he is one of our highest esteemed patriots who—by the way—deserves your utmost respect."

Hao pressed his hands to his eyes. "I don't

believe this. You gave him clearance? Just because he knows some engineers? Do you realize he signed a billion dollar contract with the United States military last month? Don't you find that a little suspicious?" His voice trailed off suddenly and his mouth fell open. "But you already knew this..."

The High Inspector humphed, clearly not in the mood for this conversation. "Canada and the United States have common goals. We have the technology; they have the manpower. It's only natural we work together."

Hao sat back and clenched his teeth. "What about the fugitives, then?"

"The ones whose bodies we never recovered from the avalanche?" the High Inspector jabbed. "What about them?"

Hao ignored the criticism and searched through the papers, then pointed at a list. "Ryan Archer, Wayne McGuillen, Susan Pickering, Thomas Nombeko... do you see any pattern here?"

The High Inspector shrugged. "No. But I'm sure you're going to tell me."

"Over the past months, our fugitives have had contacts with all *The Cosmic Fall* witnesses on this list—save one. They even sought refuge with some of them."

"So?"

Hao tried to remain patient. "So, our intel has told us the fugitives are alive and heading east." His finger slid down to the last name on the list. "And who is the last witness we know is located in the east?"

The High Inspector bent forward to look at the name. "Victor Hayward," he read.

CHAPTER 7 *Safe Haven*

The ball hit Ben square in the cheek.

"Pay attention, squirt!" Bob yelled from a distance. "Are you okay?"

Ben rubbed the side of his head. "Yeah." He picked up the soccer ball, checking his surroundings for the hundredth time, then spotted his mother. She was walking at a fast pace on the footpath that crossed Tommy Thompson Park.

Ben dropped the ball and ran over to meet her. "Did it work?"

She nodded, heading towards a tree where Ben and Bob had left their sweaters. She dropped to the ground and let out a long, shaky breath.

"Way to go, Mom!" Ben said, full of wonder.

"Is he wearing..."

"Sh!" she warned, glancing over his shoulder.

Ben turned and found Bob jogging up to them.

"Hi, baby. How was your meeting?" Bob said, out of breath.

"Exhausting," she answered, studying their green surroundings. "This is nice. I could take a nap, right here." She grabbed the sweaters, rolled them up and placed them behind her neck, then closed her eyes.

"Come on," Bob gestured to Ben. "Let's give her a breather. Three-to-one. I'm winning, squirt. Better get at it!"

He bent to pick up the ball, but Ben called after him. "Thanks, Uncle Bob, but I don't feel like playing anymore. I think I'll go for a walk."

Ben caught a brief look of disappointment on his uncle's face, but the man shrugged and showed off his soccer skills by repeatedly kicking the ball on his knee and heel.

A small buzz near Ben's ear made him raise his hand to it.

Hey! You're tickling me.

Beetrix hovered in front of his face.

You're going the wrong way, Benjamin Archer. We've searched this area already.

I know, I know. Bear with me for a minute. There's something I need to do first.

Ben pushed through some shrubs until he was satisfied that no one could see him. Then he sat, Beetrix settling on a leaf nearby, observing him.

When Mesmo had indicated the glittering diamond in the centre of his grandfather's watch, and had told him it allowed the alien to travel in spirit to Ben's location, it had never crossed Ben's mind that *he* might be the one who would, one day, need to use the device.

But could he? He had never attempted it, nor had he asked Mesmo if it was remotely possible for a human to disconnect his spirit from his physical body.

"I guess you are more than a normal Earth human now..." Mesmo had said, many months ago. Ben felt a pang of loss at the memory. He missed Mesmo more than he cared to admit.

Beetrix buzzed next to him, pulling him away from thoughts that threatened to drown him if he lingered on them for too long.

He moved restlessly, trying to find peace in body and mind. Would Mesmo realize that Victor Hayward was wearing the watch? Would Ben be able to connect to it?

The idea was completely crazy. If the plan didn't work, they risked losing contact with Mesmo for good.

Why didn't you send me?

Ben glanced at Beetrix sternly.

Don't be silly. It would have been way too dangerous. Besides, we have to find your hive.

Ben was going to close his eyes again, but he changed his mind and shot an annoyed look at the insect again.

And stay out of my thoughts!

* * *

"So, you like it here?" Bob asked as Laura opened her eyes. He was sitting close to her, smiling.

Oh boy, he still has those deep, brown eyes. Not like Mesmo's, but...

Laura rolled to a sitting position. She removed soil from her hands by wiping them together, then looked up at the trees with their fresh, spring leaves. "I could get used to living here, I guess..."

"Then do it," Bob said.

"What?"

"Live here. Permanently. With me." Seeing

the look on her face, Bob raised his eyes to the sky. "Okay, okay. Not *with* me, then. But close, so I can spend more time with Ben."

She squinted her eyes. "I hope you're not considering joint custody." It was meant as a joke, but she suddenly regretted saying the words.

Bob shrugged. "No. Yes. Maybe. Why not?" He glanced at her.

He is *thinking about it!* she realized in shock.

He crossed his hands behind his head and lay down. "Oh, I don't know. It's just that, he and I, we're bonding, you know? He's a great kid—apart from his insect craze. But that will wear off. Those things always do."

"I don't think..." Laura began.

"Just look around you, Laura. There's everything he needs here: good schools, good jobs. He'll make tons of friends. He can come work for me later. Jeez, for all I know, he could take over one day..."

"Bob, Bob!" Laura snapped. "You're daydreaming. Bounce back to reality already!"

Bob straightened. "What? Does that sound so off the beaten track? Do you still think so low of me then? I could be a great dad, you know?"

"It's not that easy," Laura seethed.

"Of course, it's not that easy. But give me a

chance to learn, Laura. Can you give me that, at least?"

Laura looked away. She felt like Ben was slipping away from her. After fighting so hard to stick together, she was finding this to be the toughest challenge she had yet faced.

Joint custody: one week with me, one week with Bob.

That's what life would look like.

I can't do it!

Her mind tripped over itself, searching for a way out.

I can't keep Ben away from his dad, either.

She was so lost in an inner debate that she didn't realize Ben had walked up to them until his shadow fell over her.

"Can we go home, now?" he said, his face looking crestfallen.

* * *

They sat on the bed opposite each other, their legs crossed, speaking in low voices so Bob wouldn't hear them.

"This isn't working, Mom," Ben said, discouraged. "Mesmo isn't connecting with me."

Laura took his hands in her own. "Be patient.

Mesmo may not have realized that Victor has the watch yet."

"What if he does, but we aren't able to make contact?"

"We talked about this. We decided it was worth a try. If it doesn't work, we'll think of something else. Let's give it a rest for now. It's late. You can try again tomorrow morning."

Ben sighed in exasperation, then lay down on the bed.

"Come on," Laura said. "Let's get some sleep."

She switched off the light and Ben stared at the dark with his eyes wide open.

"Mom?" he said softly, fighting a sudden lump in his throat.

"What?"

Around this time of night, Tike would be lying beside him—he could almost physically feel the dog's warm body. But he reached out his hand and touched only emptiness. Feeling crushed, he said, "I wish Tike were still alive. I wish that police officer hadn't shot him. I wish..."

"Shush," Laura said in a hushed voice. He heard her turn to face him. "You know, I've been meaning to tell you, I don't think that police officer meant to kill Tike. He was aiming at the grizzly. I don't think he even realized Tike was there."

"But it's not fair, Tike never hurt anybody..." Ben sobbed.

"I know, honey," she replied. "But sometimes I wonder where we'd be, if it hadn't been for that avalanche triggered by the shot..." She fell silent, then said after a while, "Ben?"

"What?" he sniffed.

"Remember when I promised you I'd find a place where we could belong?"

"Uh-huh."

"Well," she said. "What if that place was here?"

Ben raised his head from the cushion. "With Uncle Bob?"

Laura didn't answer right away, but when she did, her voice was muffled. "Maybe not *with* Uncle Bob. But nearby. He can help us settle in. Would you like that?"

Ben thought about it. He liked Uncle Bob. They had their differences, but it was like having a piece of his dad. "Maybe," he answered slowly.

"Let's sleep on it," Laura said. "You can check out your new school, and I'll give my new job a try. We can talk about it again in a week."

"After we've saved Mesmo," Ben added.

"Yes," Laura agreed. "After we've saved Mesmo."

They fell silent. Ben stared at the darkness, lost in thought.

* * *

Victor Hayward paced the floor with his head down and his hands on his hips, while a young assistant whispered the latest updates to him.

"Placing humans in an induced coma gives their body a chance to heal. But that's not the case with the alien. Every time we wake him up, he gets worse. We're running out of options."

Hayward removed his glasses and rubbed his face. "*I'm* running out of options." He paced a moment longer, then put his glasses back on. "I'm going to deal with him, once and for all."

"Boss!" the man warned, but Hayward picked up a grey object from an examination table and then scanned his badge to unlock a metal door.

When he entered the bare room, the first thing he noticed was the alien's white hair. Even observing the being from this distance in the dim light, Hayward had to admit it had a deathly look.

The businessman approached the hospital bed. He held the metallic object inches away from the subject. The object began to levitate.

The alien who lay on the hospital bed with feeding tubes sticking out of its arms opened its eyes a crack.

Hayward met the being's gaze. "I know you can hear me. So, I want you to listen closely, friend. I'm a wealthy and powerful man. I own thousands of airplanes that have crossed the world countless times.

"But the fuel we use for these airplanes is running out. If I don't find alternative energy soon, my company will go out of business. I will be forced to fire thousands of people who depend on me to feed their families..."

He gestured towards the floating object. "This piece was extracted out of your spaceship, and it reacts to you. Therefore, I believe you hold the solution to my problem."

Hayward snagged the object from the air and slipped it into his pocket. "I will ask you one final time. Tell me about the energy that fuels your craft, show me how it works, and I guarantee your freedom. I can get you on a plane by morning, to any destination you may desire."

He stopped at the end of the bed. "I can

make you a special deal, friend. This one time only." He stared at the floor, choosing the words carefully. "What if I saw to it that you could get home? You see, I have no interest in you—I'm only interested in your technology. So, help me duplicate your flying saucer, show me how it works, and I will provide you with access to your own spacecraft. Because, you see," he straightened his glasses. "I know where it is, and I can lead you to it."

The extraterrestrial hadn't moved an inch, but Hayward knew it was listening because it followed him with its eyes. The subject opened its mouth, and a sound left its lips as if it wanted to speak.

"What?" Hayward said, lifting his hand to his ear and approaching the alien's head. "Speak up!"

The being tried again, but only a croaking sound left its throat.

Hayward's adrenalin rose slightly. It was the first time he was getting a reaction. Maybe he was finally getting a breakthrough. He checked that the subject's arms and legs were firmly attached to the bedframe, then leaned forward expectantly.

Something caught at his wrist. Yelping, Hayward jerked back. But the alien had wrapped its fingers tightly around Hayward's wrist and was staring at him with intense eyes. Hayward struggled, watching in horror as the subject lifted its head, its voice coming out in rasps.

"I will not speak a good word for you," it said. The faintest trace of a smile appeared on its face, then it sank back weakly.

Hayward roared, just as his men erupted into the room. But the alien had already let him go.

The businessman rubbed at his wrist, his teeth bared. "You've sealed your fate, friend," he snarled.

As he stormed out of the room, his edgy assistant followed closely. "What did he say?"

"Baloney!"

* * *

It happened all at once. One second, Ben was fast asleep; the next, he felt a jolt and tumbled into the void. He wanted to scream, but the high velocity pushed his voice to the back of his throat. He tried to grasp on to something, but could not find his hands.

Then, as suddenly as it had begun, the sensation vanished, and he was himself again. Or at least, he thought he was.

His senses on high alert, he reached for the bed light but found only air around him. His eyes focused slowly. Soft light washed over him, then forms began to take shape.

Where am I?

A corridor, illuminated by dull night lights, stretched out before him. Several doors took shape to his left and right, while the corridor continued behind him. The door in front of him stood open.

He tried to remember where he had been last, but his thoughts were jumbled. He checked himself and found that he was in one piece, wearing pyjamas.

I must be dreaming.

Deciding to go along with this mind trick, he stepped through the door and found himself in a room filled with strange apparatus. Computer screens flashed strings of information, science jars contained mysterious liquids, baffling instruments lay strewn across a table. Ben concluded he was in some kind of laboratory.

To his right, he discovered a large window. He glanced through the smoked glass and found a dim, empty room that only contained a hospital bed. A man with white hair lay on it.

Ben gasped. "Mesmo!"

CHAPTER 8 *Contact*

Ben stepped back from the window giddily. He stared at his hands, which seemed solid, but when he tried to make them touch, they passed right through each other. His mouth fell open in exhilaration mixed with fear.

I did it!

His spirit had disconnected from his body and had travelled to Mesmo's location, at the alien's call.

Mesmo has the spirit portal!

He turned to the window again.

I have to tell him I'm here.

Loud voices filled the corridor.

Tensing in dismay, the boy searched for a hiding spot, then dove frantically behind a filing cabinet in the nick of time, just before two men entered the room. Ben heard them close the door, then settle in front of their computers on the opposite side of a lab table.

Making sure they were concentrated on their work, Ben crawled behind the lab table to the door, then reached for the doorknob. His fingers slipped through it.

Drat!

He checked on the men hurriedly, and instead found a security camera in a top corner of the room, aimed in his direction. A green light flickered on it. Beside him, several screens projected images from other security cameras. Mesmo was visible on one of these screens, a wobbly, static image of Ben on another.

He retreated with his back to the lab table and shut his eyes tight.

Think!

To begin with, he couldn't save Mesmo. Not in his spirit state. What he needed to do was find out Mesmo's location. He checked his surroundings for any clues but found none.

I'm going to have to inspect the whole facility.

Ben closed his eyes again, trying to accept that the laws of physics had changed now that he was intangible. He opened his eyes to study the door, and, instead, found himself in the same room as Mesmo.

* * *

Victor Hayward considered his options while he brushed his teeth. As he pushed out the toothpaste, he considered the pros and cons of delivering the subject to the American military. Or, he could start a bidding war between major world powers. It would pay off a good deal of his debts. If only he had been able to make the alien talk, things would have been so much easier, but that alternative was fading fast.

The important thing was to keep the Canadians out of it. They had, after all, stolen the spaceships off his land, claiming it was "federal property."

"Federal property," he snorted with a mouth full of bubbles.

"What, sweetheart?" his wife called from the bedroom.

He spat into the sink. "Nothing, dear. I'm talking to myself."

He got back to brushing his teeth, mulling over the idea, but he didn't like it. The extraterrestrial was *his*. He had caught the alien. Not the CSIS, not MI6, not the KGB. Not any of those secret services, but *he*, Victor Hayward—because *he* was the one who had discovered the alien lying among the debris of the crash.

Hayward quickly dismissed the uncomfortable memory of his first contact with the being. He had approached it, thinking it dead. But when the alien had moved its head, Hayward had shrieked and run for his life. Not one of his finest moments, he had to admit.

Fortunately, the alien's facial traits had been burned into his mind—enough for him to send out a quiet face recognition search among his Victory Air crew across the globe, with a positive outcome.

For goodness sake! This creature had been travelling the world doing God-knows-what since its arrival. If not for Hayward, it would most likely still be going about its business with complete impunity.

He filled his cheeks with water and pressed on his phone to pull up the security screens of his underground laboratory, his toothbrush still in his hand.

That's when he saw the boy.

He gagged on the water in his mouth.

"Are you okay, sweetheart?" his wife called while he coughed raucously into the sink.

He rushed into the bedroom—toothpaste stuck to the side of his mouth—and jumped into a pair of trousers and shirt.

"Sweetheart?"

He left his startled wife, grabbed his phone and jacket and practically flew down the stairs of his mansion. He swung open the front door, struggled to put on his coat, then dialled a number on the phone while sprinting towards his limousine.

When he knocked loudly on the windowpane, his chauffeur—who was fast asleep in the driver's seat—jumped so hard Hayward thought he was going to have a heart attack. The man scrambled to catch the hat that slipped off his head, then clumsily extracted himself from the vehicle.

Hayward's cellphone was stuck to his ear, ringing on the other end. He heard a click as his assistant picked up.

"A boy! There's a boy in the room with the alien!" Hayward screamed into the receiver.

He grabbed the chauffeur's car keys and pushed him aside. "Move over!" he yelled, plunging into the car, then turned on the ignition and screeched away into the night.

* * *

Forgetting his own safety, Ben rushed to the hospital bed and found the alien extended on it. Mesmo's cheekbones protruded through his grey skin. Gone was his friend's rock solid frame.

Ben held back a cry.

What if he's... dying?

The alien turned his sunken eyes to him and managed a small smile. "Benjamin," he whispered, opening his hand. The watch with the spirit portal rested in his palm.

"It worked!" Ben gasped, though he had to muster up the courage to speak.

Has Mesmo been in this state all this time?

Could Mesmo make his spirit appear healthy and strong, while in fact, his physical body ailed? Ben didn't dare think of the answer.

"I'm here now," he said encouragingly. "Don't worry, I'll get you out. I just need to figure out where we are."

A phone rang outside the room. Ben heard the man's voice who answered it turn to alarm. There was a thump and the sound of running feet.

"Go!" Mesmo urged. "You are a spirit. You

can go anywhere, as long as you stay in the vicinity of the portal."

Ben nodded, his eyes wide. "Hang in there, Mesmo," he begged.

He turned, closed his eyes and headed straight for the wall. When he opened them again, he was standing in the corridor once more, the two men staring at him from the lab door, mouths agape.

"Get him!" one of them yelled.

Ben turned and sprinted down the corridor, the men's heavy shoes thudding behind him. He headed for a door with a red EXIT sign on top of it, raised his arm and plunged, expecting to crash straight into it. Instead, he landed on the other side, unharmed.

Sooo cool! ...I think?

He hiccupped in nervous excitement. He could have sworn his spirit body was covered in goosebumps at the idea that he was passing through physical objects. But there was no time to analyze the idea.

The men pushed against the emergency exit door behind him.

Ben clambered up several flights of stairs—his pursuers huffing loudly behind him—until he found a sign that said 1ST FLOOR.

Charging head-first through the door like a bull, Ben suddenly found himself in an enormous reception area. The massive, red symbol of Victory Air ornamented the back wall. A night guard stood behind a reception desk, talking to a group of police officers who wore jackets with the letters CSIS on the back. In their midst, stood Bordock.

Ben froze.

The two men burst through the emergency exit behind him.

All groups faced each other, their eyes wide.

Ben didn't wait for them to come to their senses. He dashed over the marble floor—the hall erupting with warning shouts around him—and slipped through the main doors to the outside world. Taking refuge behind a column at the foot of an extended flight of stairs, he shut his eyes tight.

Take me back, Mesmo! Take me back!

Panic engulfed him as threatening voices neared his futile hiding spot.

There was a whoosh of air, and the ground beneath him fell. His spirit connected to his body with a bang. He yelled as if someone had just hit him with a hammer.

"Ben?" Laura's shrill voice called him in the

dark.

The bed light came on, and Ben found himself sitting upright, gasping for breath.

"Ben! What is it?" Laura cried.

He cast a distressed look her way and burst, "We have to get Mesmo out, *NOW!*"

CHAPTER 9 *Deliverance*

Laura ran into the middle of the road to hail a passing taxi cab. The driver barely had time to hit the brakes, the bumper ending so close to her that its headlights illuminated dust rising in front of her jacket.

She gestured for Ben to get into the car, and soon they were racing down Toronto streets towards the Victory Air headquarters.

It didn't take long for them to get there, and as they neared the building, the red and blue lights of half a dozen police cars became visible from afar.

"Stop here!" Laura ordered the taxi driver. She threw several dollar bills at him and clambered out after Ben. They both hurried closer to the scene of the tumult.

"What should we do?" Ben asked worriedly.

"We'll have to find another way in," she said. "Maybe through that service street there."

"No, wait!" Ben held her back. "I have a better idea."

* * *

Victor Hayward's phone continued to ring. He had no intention of answering, his eyes were glued to the road before him as he sped into town way over the speed limit. But the phone rang again, and when he glanced at it, he realized it was his assistant. He picked it up at the risk of ending in a ditch.

"What?"

"Boss, the police are here."

"The what?" he bellowed.

His assistant's voice wavered. "Yes, Boss. The CSIS is here with a warrant to search the building. They say they are searching for proof that we knew our oil extraction fields were depleted."

Hayward snorted into the phone. "Yeah, right! Bunch of liars. They know we have the 'package.' Resort to Plan B. I want the 'package' removed at once. You have two minutes. Do you understand?"

His assistant sounded distant and nervous. "Yes, Boss. Removing 'the package' at once."

* * *

Ben decided he wasn't enjoying this spirit travelling much. He'd much rather soar on a bird's wings or dive into the deep on the back of a whale, but right now he had no choice.

He wasn't sure where he would end up, or even if Mesmo was up to the task of connecting with him, but as soon as he focused on the alien, his spirit jolted out of his body and materialized in an underground parking.

Hearing voices, Ben hid behind a car and watched as Mesmo was rolled on the hospital bed into a waiting ambulance. They caught sight of each other for an instant before the ambulance doors were shut on him.

Pursing his lips, Ben noticed the ramp that the vehicle would use to escape—and he instantly knew what he needed to do.

* * *

The limo screeched to a stop. Victor Hayward exited the vehicle and ran up meticulous stairs to the entrance of his headquarters. He pulled the doors wide open, making sure his voice boomed into the reception. "What's going on here?"

His short legs took him to the dozen-or-so police officers who were assembled under the red symbol of his company.

A man detached himself from the group. He was not wearing the CSIS vest like the others, but a neat, light-grey suit that Hayward would have approved of in other circumstances. A sense of authority hung around the agent. The lights reflected on his shaved head but not in his emotionless green eyes. Either way, Hayward knew instinctively that he had to tread with care— he recognized a person with his level of intellect when he saw one.

"Mr. Hayward?" the bald man said, showing him a piece of identification. "I'm Agent Theodore Connelly, with the National Aerial Division of the Canadian Security Intelligence Service. We have a search warrant for the premises."

"Naturally," Hayward growled icily, noting that Mister Bigshot here wasn't even hiding which department he was working for. *He can wipe his nose on his search warrant for all I care—as long as he doesn't find the alien...*

"Mr. Hayward, I need to talk to you privately," the agent said.

Whatever keeps them busy, Hayward thought. Out loud, he said, "Follow me."

Agent Connelly gestured for his men to spread out and Hayward noted with satisfaction that they were heading to the elevators, which he knew—did not go down to his secret, underground laboratory. A makeshift laboratory, for sure, but one he had had the visionary presence of mind to build after witnessing The Cosmic Fall. Only one separate elevator connected to it from the reception—and he had the key.

Both men entered the room that the receptionists used to work in when they weren't out front.

Hayward leaned against a desk and crossed his arms. "Well? Let's have it. What's this all about?"

Connelly closed the office door, and when he faced Hayward, he wasn't smiling. The agent's eyes bored into him. "Mr. Hayward," Connelly said in a low, threatening voice. "You have exactly two minutes to deliver the alien to me."

Hayward's arms dropped, as did his mouth. "Wha...?" But his voice caught in his throat because something entirely abnormal was happening to Connelly's face.

* * *

Ben raced up the ramp of the underground parking area. Far below him, the ambulance roared to life. He ignored the closed garage door and dashed through it, finding himself in a dark service street close to where Laura and his physical self were located.

It took him a few seconds to find what he was looking for.

"Please let this work, please, please, please," he begged, as tires squealed up the ramp of the garage door behind him.

Ben hid beside it and waited.

* * *

Connelly called for reinforcements as he headed for a separate elevator located not far from the receptionist's office. It was locked with a security system.

Unfazed, Connelly pulled out the security

card Hayward had given him willingly only moments ago as he begged for his life. Connelly scanned it and the elevator door opened, allowing him to head down to the level indicated by Hayward.

The shapeshifter glanced left and right at the corridor that appeared before him. He headed to the right, finding an open door at the end which led to a laboratory.

His sharp ears caught the sound of distant, screeching tires. He tensed, then doubled back and searched for the source of the noise.

* * *

The garage door lifted slowly, the driver of the ambulance pressing on the gas pedal impatiently, making the motor roar.

The door had barely raised when the vehicle lurched forward into the service street, which was closed at one end. It turned left with the intention of joining city traffic.

Only, a young boy stood right in its path.

The driver swerved so hard that the ambulance swayed and collided into a fire hydrant located at the exit. The jet of water that was released upon impact was so powerful that it enveloped the ambulance under a swirling waterfall.

Ben watched expectantly.

It didn't take long. The flow slowed and hardened, turning to ice in answer to Mesmo's skill. It crackled and gleamed under the street lights, its churning form caught in time.

Ben heard shouts coming from inside the ambulance. The driver struggled with the door, which resisted under the weight of the ice. It finally gave way with a loud crunch, allowing him to make his escape.

But Ben had stopped watching. He closed his eyes and returned to his physical body with a jolt.

"Ben!" Laura called from far away. He groaned at the force with which his spirit reconnected to his body.

"Get up! Hurry!" Laura half lifted, half dragged him to a standing position.

He became aware of a grating sound. He focused his eyes and ears and found the back doors of the ambulance opening with difficulty, scraping at the ice that surrounded it. Four men, who shouted frantically to each other, spilled out and scampered away, while water continued to flow from the fire hydrant, flooding the street.

Ben and Laura approached the opening at

the back of the ambulance. Just then, the shadow of a man appeared, making them gasp. The man stepped into the light. His white hair was disheveled, the tone of his skin light-grey.

"Mesmo!" Ben cried with relief.

The alien slumped against the side of the ambulance.

Ben and Laura reached out to him. He made to step down, but his legs gave way, and he toppled forward out of the van. Ben and Laura almost collapsed as he fell into their arms, but they managed to hold on just long enough for him to regain his balance. Laura swung one of his arms over her shoulders, Ben hurriedly trying to do the same, but the alien's height meant he wasn't much help. Still, shifting his weight between them, Mesmo managed to hunker forward, groaning painfully.

The three of them hugged the shadows and made their escape.

* * *

Connelly sprinted up the garage ramp, anxious to discover the origin of the racket outside. He found the ambulance wrapped up in a small iceberg at the end of the service alley, with water flooding the main street.

The shapeshifter rushed to the vehicle's back doors and peered inside. It was empty. He balled his fists and hit the floor of the vehicle so hard it left a dent. His body shook with fury. His eyes switched colour as he struggled to keep Connelly's appearance under the weight of his anger.

Running footsteps approached behind him, and it took all of his willpower to contain himself. If he turned around now, he would explode.

"What's going on? Is anyone hurt?" a man asked, bumping into him as he tried to glimpse over Connelly's shoulder into the ambulance.

The shapeshifter shut his eyes tight.

Some more men arrived. "Agent Connelly? What are your orders?"

Connelly inhaled deeply through his nostrils. He opened his green eyes slowly and was about to respond when he noticed an object at the base of the hospital bed which lay overturned on the floor of the ambulance. He reached for the object and his hand closed on a silver watch.

At first, Connelly couldn't believe his luck, but the way the tiny diamond shone in its centre was unmistakable.

"Agent Connelly?"

Police sirens whirled to a stop behind him,

and more people gathered around the ambulance.

Connelly clasped the watch tightly and smirked.

CHAPTER 10 *Arrest*

Ben and Laura shoved Mesmo into a doorway just in time to avoid the headlights of a passing police car. Ben peeked out of their hiding place to make sure it didn't turn back, then let out his breath as the swirling lights faded away.

"Let's go!" he urged, glancing at his mother and the alien. His mouth fell open.

Wait a minute! Are they kissing?

Had he just caught Mesmo and Laura in an embrace? He couldn't be sure, because his mother pulled back with an incredulous look on her face.

"Hey! Time to go!" Ben tugged at his mother's arm.

She blinked at him, then placed Mesmo's arm around her shoulder again. "Come on. Bob's condo is just a block away."

They stepped onto the sidewalk, but Mesmo dropped to his knees, almost dragging her down with him. "No!" he gasped. "Outside. Water."

Ben exchanged a worried look with his mother. His mind whirled. "Let's take him to the park! It's not far."

Laura nodded. "Good idea. You can make it, Mesmo."

Ben couldn't avoid staring at the alien's face. It was drawn, his skin almost as grey as Kaia's had been...

...when she died.

He took Mesmo by the arm and stared at the man with intense determination.

You can't die.

As if reading Ben's mind, Mesmo set his jaw and forced himself up.

The dark outline of trees came into view some painstaking minutes later. It took all of Laura and Ben's strength to haul the tall man through the wooded park. They grunted under his weight and had to pause every now and then so Mesmo could lift his head and take in a deep mouthful of fresh air.

The sound of tiny, lapping waves reached Ben's ears. Mesmo must have heard it, too, because his pace quickened. They broke through some bushes and found themselves at the edge of a short beach that led to Lake Ontario.

Mesmo let go of them. He stumbled forward, walking straight into the water without slowing down.

Laura reached out her hand as if wanting to hold him back, but remained by Ben's side. They watched the alien wade up to his knees into the lake. He paused, then let himself drop face first into the water like a rigid plank. The dark liquid submerged him until only rings on the surface indicated where he had stood.

Ben shadowed his mother's footsteps as they hurried to the edge, searching the darkness for his presence. They waited, the seconds ticking by in slow motion.

"There!" Laura whispered suddenly, pointing to her right.

A barely visible glow moved under the water but became stronger as it glided to a standstill some distance before them. Then it approached the surface, and Mesmo's head broke through the water. He looked in their direction, a bluish halo emanating from his body.

Ben watched, astonished.

Woman and boy stood by the edge, slightly

out of breath, wondering what would happen next.

Then, to Ben's utter surprise, Mesmo threw his head back and laughed. It was a strong, heartfelt sound that caught him completely off guard. It resonated through the night, open and sincere.

I've never heard Mesmo laugh before.

Ben cast his mother a quizzical look.

Laura frowned at him with the same wonder reflected in her eyes, while a smile crept on to her face.

Ben couldn't contain a grin, his nervousness overcome by a sudden sense of pride at what they had accomplished.

We did it!

The thought made his whole body tingle. After all their hardships and turmoil, they had done it! They had freed Mesmo. He chuckled at the realization, though Mesmo's elation fueled the rising feeling inside of him.

Beside him, Laura's timid giggle turned into real laughter, and before long, she cracked up completely.

Ben followed her lead, whooping loudly into the night, letting go of months of bottled up emotions, thrilled at the idea that they had outsmarted both Victor Hayward *and* Bordock, not to mention an overwhelming relief at being together for real at last.

He let it all go and found himself splashing, fully dressed, into the lake to join Mesmo. The water enveloped him in a warm blanket, glowing a soft blue in response to the alien's skill. Ben threw himself into Mesmo's arms, his tears of laughter turning into emotional ones.

Mesmo became silent, then wrapped his own arms around the boy.

They remained like that for a while, Ben feeling slightly bewildered at hugging the alien in flesh and bone for the first time.

* * *

"You should eat something," the nurse said. She placed a food tray next to Hao's bed.

"Yes, yes," Hao replied impatiently, as he typed away at the computer on his lap.

The nurse remained by his side, but the Inspector was so absorbed by his work that it took him a while to acknowledge her.

Finally, he looked up, then at the tray. "Yes, yes, I'll eat," he insisted, grabbing a piece of toast and stuffing it in his mouth.

The nurse pressed her lips into a fine line, then exited the hospital room.

Hao got back to his screen, his cheeks full, then reached out for a folder on the side of his bed.

The room lay littered with boxes, files and documents from *The Cosmic Fall.* If the High Inspector got wind of this, Hao would be in deep trouble. But at this point, he didn't care. After all, he had set the High Inspector on Victor Hayward's track and was waiting for news of the raid on the businessman's headquarters.

As he picked up the folder, his eyes fell on the TV which was constantly streaming news.

VICTORY AIR—CEO ARRESTED, the red banner at the bottom of the screen read.

Hao left the piece of toast dangling from the side of his mouth and reached hurriedly for the control to turn up the volume.

"...in what investigators claim to be the biggest fraud in the country's history. The founder of Victory Air and owner of the billion-dollar industry responsible for extracting oil for the airliner is accused of having lied about the years of resources still available in Alberta. It is thought the tar sand oil was depleted over four years ago, and that, instead, Mr. Hayward redirected substantial Federal funding—destined to modernize the industry—to the United States, where he obtained the fuel for his airliner, thus avoiding bankruptcy..." the reporter explained.

Hao munched slowly as he watched cameras flashing at the businessman who was being led down the stairs of his Toronto building. The man's face was ashen. His eyes were glazed and unresponsive to the shouting reporters around him.

A police officer wearing a CSIS vest helped Victor Hayward into the back of a police car.

The phone next to Hao's bed rang. He reached out for it, groaning as he twisted his broken leg.

His assistant's voice said, "You were right. The extraterrestrial was here. We have footage from security cameras..."

"What do you mean *was?*" Hao barked.

"We think the fugitives helped the alien escape just before we arrived. We're combing the city for them as we speak."

Hao's knuckles went white as he grasped at the bedsheets. But he said in a calm tone, "Send me the footage as soon as you can."

"Yes, Sir."

Hao hung up. He stared at the TV without

really seeing it. He should have been there. The High Inspector had put Connelly in charge of the raid, but his partner had not been up to the task.

Hao carefully slid his cast leg to the edge of the bed, so he was in a sitting position. There were so many unanswered questions. What was the relationship between the fugitives and Victor Hayward? What was the alien doing there? And then there was the question of the boy, Benjamin Archer.

Hao stared at two contradicting documents laid out on the bed. One contained the blood results from the boy, proving the child was not human. The other was a birth certificate recently uncovered at a hospital on the West Coast. In it, the hospital declared the birth of a healthy, *normal* boy. There had been no mention of a father.

How could the hospital not have noticed anything unusual? How could an alien child have been hiding in plain sight among humans for so long? And if an alien child could be born in a hospital undetected, how many more were out there?

There were too many inconsistencies in this whole investigation, and Hao did not like inconsistencies. He wanted clear, logical answers.

His eyes fell on the box labelled WITNESSES. He had put a team of researchers on to each witness, they had dug up every last detail on these peoples' lives, but only Victor Hayward had given any result.

A name stuck out of one of the folders in the box: THEODORE EDMOND CONNELLY: the only one who had not undergone the same rigorous investigation as the other witnesses. Seeing as Connelly was a police officer, all had automatically assumed that his testimony was reliable.

But what if it wasn't?

Hao set his jaw and pulled out Connelly's file.

* * *

Laura caressed Ben's hair. The boy had fallen asleep with his head on her lap. Laura sat, cross-legged, on the little beach that bordered Lake Ontario, watching Mesmo as he floated in the water, staring up at the night sky.

Laura glanced up as well and let her eyes adjust until stars became visible. She would have liked to stay like this for hours. Everything was peaceful; an almost imperceptible breeze moved the leaves of the trees above her, the water lapped quietly at the shore, and a comfortable warmth enveloped her.

But the crack of dawn neared with every passing minute, and she knew the city would wake up soon. She shook Ben's shoulder gently. "Wake up, honey. We should go."

He moaned and rolled off her lap into a sitting position, then rubbed his eyes.

They both stood and approached the edge of the lake, while Mesmo straightened, still submerged in the water.

"We have to go, Mesmo," Laura said. "The park's going to be full of joggers and people walking their dogs in an hour."

"You go," the alien agreed. "I'll stay here. I need time to recover and this is the perfect place for me." He let himself sink into the water to show them that he could hide easily.

When he emerged again, Laura asked worriedly, "Are you sure?"

Mesmo nodded. "I'm sure. It's you two who have to be careful. You're the ones who are out in the open."

"We'll be fine," Laura said. "We're safe with Bob."

They agreed to meet that afternoon.

"I'm going to dye your hair," Laura said. "You won't make it very far looking like that." She pointed at his white, wavy hair.

Laura and Ben said their goodbyes, then slipped through the park.

Laura plodded behind Ben in semi-darkness, fighting off the morning chill that seeped into her clothes.

Suddenly Ben stopped. Laura bumped into him.

"Shh!" he said, raising his hand in warning.

"What is it?" she asked hurriedly.

They stood still, listening to the rustling leaves and far away sound of cars.

"I don't hear anyth..." she began, but Ben raised his hand higher.

He stepped slowly towards a compact group of shrubs, Laura following closely behind with her heart thumping. Behind the bushes, she found a small, arched bridge made of bricks. A stream trickled under it. Ben headed for it.

She was about to ask what on Earth he was doing when she noticed the sound. It was faint at first, but the closer she got to the bridge, the louder it became.

It was a humming sound, one that she recognized immediately. A buzz whisked by her ear, then several others, and soon she found herself surrounded by a cloud of insects.

"Bees!" she exclaimed.

Ben grinned. "Beetrix' hive," he confirmed.

* * *

"Hello? Is this Tamara Connelly?" Hao spoke into the phone. Connelly's file lay open before him, and he stared at the picture that was clipped to the side. It showed a youthful woman with curly hair and a dark-skinned face. Her smile revealed neat, white teeth. Even from this single picture, Hao got a sense of a fundamentally confident and happy person.

He hadn't seen the picture since his meeting with Connelly and the High Inspector months ago, when they had first been assigned to *The Cosmic Fall* case.

The woman who answered the phone did not reflect any trace of confidence or happiness in her voice, and Hao could hear a baby crying in the background. "Connelly?" the woman said scornfully. "I don't go by that name anymore. Who's this, anyway?"

Hao cleared his throat. "I'm sorry to bother you, Miss. My name is Inspector James Hao. I'm with the CSIS."

The baby's cries became louder but then died down, and Hao could hear it cooing near the receiver.

"What do you want?" Tamara asked curtly.

"I'm calling about your husband, Theodore Edmond Connelly."

To his surprise, Tamara cackled darkly. *"Theodore?* He lets you call him that?"

Hao knit his brow. "Excuse me?"

Tamara sighed. "Anyone close to Ted knows not to call him Theodore. He'd punch you in the nose if you dared utter that name. He hates it! Says it makes him sound like an old uncle or something." Her voice faltered.

"Mr. Hao, have you heard from my husband? I've called your office hundreds of times. They won't patch me through. He hasn't spoken to me since that crazy meteor business. He's literally disappeared off the face of the Earth! And I can't live like this anymore, Mr. Hao."

The baby began crying again. "Hold on," she said.

Hao heard her shushing the baby, then her voice came through again. "What was it you were calling about again?"

Hao searched for the right words. "Oh, er, I

was calling to let you know that your husband is doing a great service to his country..."

"Are you serious?" Tamara blew up. The baby cried in the background again. "I had a baby girl two months ago, Mr. Hao. Are you listening to me? Ted became a father for the second time, and he hasn't come home once to meet her!"

Hao heard her burst into tears. It took her several minutes to calm down.

She sniffed and said with a broken voice, "It's just not like him. We were happy, before. But I've had enough! You can tell him I want those divorce papers signed. I'm tired of waiting. Goodbye, Mr. Hao."

He thought she would hang up, but instead, she added. "And tell him... tell him, if he won't talk to me, to at least call his son Kyle for his fifth birthday. It's the day after tomorrow, April third." Her voice broke again. "That's the least he could do."

Silence fell between them, Hao at a loss for words. Then he heard a click, and the line went dead.

CHAPTER 11 *Light Years*

"Well, hi there, lazy heads," Bob said.

Laura entered the living room, following Ben who rubbed his hair and yawned. Bright sunlight seeped into the apartment.

Bob was sitting on the sofa with one foot resting on the coffee table, his hand on the TV control. "I thought you'd never get up. It's two in the afternoon! Were you partying all night or what? I heard you come in at dawn."

Ben glanced at Laura.

"We met up with an old friend," Laura said quickly. "We had a lot of catching up to do."

"I see. The friend with a cat name, huh?"

Laura opened her mouth to answer, but Bob had already lost interest and was pointing the control at the TV. "Hey, didn't your dad know this guy, Victor Hayward?"

Laura tensed and stared at the screen. They watched as the pale businessman was led away by police in front of the Victory Air building.

He looks like he's seen a ghost!

Even Laura could tell there was something going on with the man. But there was no time to analyze the thought because Victor Hayward's image was replaced by one of Mesmo.

POLICE SEARCHING FOR CRIMINAL IN CENTRAL TORONTO, the caption read.

The image was a grainy one. Mesmo's high cheekbones, square chin and straight nose, along with his white hair, was unmistakable.

Laura slipped in front of the TV. "Victor Hayward?" she said. "Yes, I think that was my parent's neighbour back home. I don't remember, really." Anxious to change the subject, she asked, "So, what are your plans for today?"

Bob sighed, switched off the television and said, "I know it's Saturday, but I've got to head into work for a couple of hours. Want to meet up at the park later?"

Laura straightened some cushions nonchalantly, while Bob picked up his jacket that hung from a kitchen stool. "Uh, I think Ben and I are going to stay here and rest," she answered. "Monday's a big day, you know? With school and work starting..."

Bob cast her an annoyed glance. "I was hoping to take you guys out for dinner. I know this really great place."

Laura's heart did a double flip. She knew why he wanted to take them out.

"How about we do that next Saturday? Let's see how things work out with the new job and school first. Then we can celebrate," she said.

Bob finished straightening his jacket while he stared at her.

Laura swallowed.

He's becoming impatient.

Bob picked up his keys and wallet and said, "Right. Saturday it is then." He pressed the button of the penthouse elevator. The doors swung open, and he disappeared inside, without saying goodbye.

Laura let out a long breath of air.

Ben came up behind her. "Mom, but I don't want to stay here. I need to go to the park." He held up his hand; the queen bee rested on it.

She nodded. "I know, so do I," she said. "I just wanted to keep Bob away from the park, now that Mesmo is all over the news. While you take care of Beetrix, I'm going to bring Mesmo some of Bob's clothes and dye his hair; otherwise he's going to stick out like a sore thumb."

* * *

Laura placed a towel over Mesmo's back to prevent the hair colour from staining his clothes. She checked that the creamy substance was spread out evenly over his hair, then nodded satisfactorily to herself as she sat beside him.

The warm afternoon had attracted crowds to the park, forcing them to search for a more secluded area near the lake. They had found a spot behind some boulders and a patch of sand long enough that they could sit with their legs stretched out.

She observed the alien closely and found his skin to be a healthier olive tan. The sun on his face was going to help a great deal, too. But it was clear he had lost a lot of weight while in captivity. Her stomach tightened at the idea he had been cooped up for so long inside four walls—something his people could not cope with, he had said.

He must have realized she was staring at him because he turned his honey-brown eyes her way.

"How are you holding up?" she asked, trying

not to blush.

He smiled, laughter lines creasing at the corner of his eyes. She realized he must have been a fundamentally cheerful person before his troubles began. "Better, thanks to you," he replied.

She smiled back. "So, what's going to happen now?" she asked softly.

He didn't let go of her eyes.

Feeling giddy, she had to force herself not to look away.

"Now, Laura Archer," he said. "You will go on your way, and I will go on with mine."

She swallowed and was unable to speak for a while. "What about Ben's skill?" she asked finally, pretending not to be affected by his words.

"What about it? It is Ben's, now. He can use it as he pleases."

Laura frowned. "You don't want it anymore, then?"

"It was never mine to want. Ben provided the information I needed, that is all."

"Yes, he told me. The animals are sick and at risk of dying out." She stared at the ground uneasily, afraid to analyze the thought. "That night, when we saw the Northern Lights, you said, something. You said 'We cannot invade what is already ours.' Does the Earth belong to the

Toreq?" She knew her voice was coming out a little too anxious, but she couldn't help it; the idea that aliens were secretly running the planet gave her goosebumps.

His smile did not reflect her concern. He picked up a twig and planted it in the sand. "Your species has a strange habit. You believe that, when you plant a stick with a flag into the ground, the surrounding land suddenly belongs to you." He drew a wide circle in the sand around the twig.

"You create borders that only exist in your mind, as if physical walls were separating one country from another, as if a flowing river, a passing rabbit or a branch from a tree belonged to one place or another, depending which side of the wall it was on. These borders change over time, depending on where you place the stick with a flag. It is a strange concept that makes no sense to me, considering that you are one and the same species living on one and the same planet."

He placed another twig on the circle and drew another circle around it—knocking down the first twig.

"If the Toreq were to apply this theory, then yes, you could say that the Earth belongs to us, because we were the first civilized beings to 'plant a flag' into your soil, before the era of the great giants."

"Before the dinosaurs...?" Laura gasped.

Mesmo nodded. "Fortunately, the Toreq do not abide by your old-fashioned flag theory. And besides," he smiled, "the Earth is a pebble with limited resources, lost in the confines of space, isolated from any cluster of civilized planets. There is nothing of interest to the Toreq here."

Laura shuddered, her arms and legs feeling woozy at the idea that humans were stuck on a lonely speck of rock in the great void of space. "And yet, here you are..."

He wiped away the sandy circles with his hand and nodded. "And yet, here I am." His eyes bore into hers, and her mouth went dry. "We simply like to keep track of the development of advanced species."

Laura bent her knees and wrapped her arms around them, shivering in spite of the sun on her skin. "Maybe that's why you always make me and Ben feel safe," she said, thinking out loud.

Mesmo frowned. "What do you mean?"

Laura shrugged. "I guess it feels good to know we're not the only ones out there. Plus, you know all these things. It's as if you could predict our future and give us a heads-up warning before we strayed too much. If only you could stay and help."

She felt him tense ever so slightly, so she changed the subject quickly. "Then, there's my asthma and Ben's panic attacks. They seem to have evaporated since we met you. I wonder why that is?"

Mesmo smiled. "You never really suffered from them," he said. "It is your mind that is convincing you that you suffer from these illnesses. But when you feel secure, you forget that you are supposed to show the symptoms. The Toreq have long learned to suppress certain illnesses with their minds. It will be a while yet before you learn to do the same. But I guess you and Ben are unconsciously following the right path already."

Laura cocked her head, unsure she believed him, but she said, "If only there were time, to get to know your people better, under friendlier circumstances. You have so much to teach, and we, so much to learn."

* * *

An hour later, Laura and Mesmo ventured out in the open among picnicking families in the park.

She checked on the alien regularly, trying to decide whether he was fit to walk among humans, and found that his now dark-brown hair, jeans and matching brown sweater with a three buttoned mock neck was more than satisfactory, even if—she had to admit—Bob's clothes were a bit small for his tall stature.

She led him to the spot where Ben had found the hive. They made their way through the thick shrubs which had grown around the unused, rundown pedestrian bridge.

Reaching the clearing, Laura gaped at the sight before her.

Ben stood in the centre of the open space, at the foot of the bridge. Sunlight seeped through the trees, illuminating him. But what made Laura start was the dense swarm of bees that circled around him, while he held out glowing blue hands to them.

Laura stayed glued to the spot, mesmerized by this surreal vision of her son. He seemed oblivious to their presence, in what appeared to be a deep conversation, until the intense buzzing dissipated, and she realized the insect frenzy was dying down.

The glow around Ben's hands diminished, the sun dipped further behind the trees and the bees zoomed by Laura's ears, away from the clearing.

Ben dropped his hands to his side, and his eyes lost their glaze as if he were once more becoming conscious of his surroundings. He turned to face Laura and Mesmo and said, "They say there is only silence."

By *they*, Laura figured he was talking about the bees. She approached him. "What do you mean?" Ben looked different, she thought. More determined, less overwhelmed by using his new skill.

I'm the one who has to get used to it now, she realized.

Ben held out his hand, and Beetrix landed on it. "They are able to communicate with other hives over great distances," he continued. "Their senses are so developed that they can capture the vibrations produced by other bee colonies located miles away. But they say now there is only silence. They feel lost and alone. Beetrix says this common web of vibrations is like life itself to them. Without it, they become confused and depressed."

Laura stared at the peanut-sized bee in Ben's hand. "What can we do?" she breathed.

"It's worse, actually," Ben said. "Beetrix says

her hive is poisoned. She has lost many bees already. She's afraid other hives may have suffered the same fate."

"Poisoned?" Laura repeated, a heavy realization seeping into her mind.

Ben nodded. "...by the flowers they feed on. She thinks the very thing they need to survive on is the one that is slowly killing them. How can that be?"

Laura rubbed at her brow. "Beetrix is right," she said, feeling ashamed to be the one telling Ben the news. "I've read about it. Apparently, millions of hives are disappearing across the globe because of something called Colony Collapse Disorder. Worker bees in a colony have been disappearing, leaving behind their queen. There is no explanation for it, but it's thought that it has to do with the pesticides we use and the loss of bee habitat from our sprawling cities." She paused.

"The problem is serious, Ben. You see, bees pollinate all types of flowers from which fruits and vegetables emerge. That's food that humans depend on."

Ben's mouth fell open. "You mean, no bees... no food...?"

Laura nodded. "Pretty much. You wouldn't think such a tiny animal could have such a big impact. But entire crops have been lost because there were no bees to pollinate them."

Ben stared at Beetrix, who buzzed her wings while remaining on his hand. "Beetrix' hive is not yet lost. Her worker bees are still here. She can be saved." He kept his eyes on the queen bee and said determinedly, "I'll save you."

Laura put her arm around his shoulders. "We can Google local beekeepers and ask for their advice. But right now, it's getting late. Let's go home."

She glanced at Mesmo as they walked by. He had been standing silently behind her the whole time. There was something in his eyes, something she couldn't quite put her finger on. Was it sadness? Or a longing for hope?

It only took them two minutes to return to the bustling side of the park, where parents were gathering their picnic boxes and their children. It wasn't summer yet, and the spring air tended to cool down by early evening.

"I thought you guys were staying home?" a voice said behind them.

Laura whirled to find Bob walking up to them. She caught him casting a sullen look Mesmo's way. He stopped before them, the muscles on his neck twitching tightly.

There was no way around this, so Laura cleared her throat. "Oh, hi, Bob. I'd like you to meet our friend, Mesmo. Mesmo, this is Bob. He's..." she trailed off.

"He's my uncle," Ben jumped in.

Bob scowled at Mesmo, then reached out to shake his hand. "Mesmo, huh?" he said with a slight edge in his voice. "I hear you're visiting?"

Laura bit her lip as she exchanged a glance with Ben.

Mesmo nodded, staying eye-level with Bob. "Yes, and I'll be on my way again, soon."

Suddenly Ben wrapped his arms around the tall man. "Don't go yet," he said. "Please."

Mesmo tipped his head to the side, then placed his hand on Ben's shoulder. "No," he said gently. "Not just yet." His eyes fell on Laura, who felt heat rising to her cheeks.

"Come on, Ben," she said quickly. "I'm sure Mesmo has things to do. And you have school to prepare for."

I need to break this up, pronto!

Addressing Bob, she said, "Shall we go?" She slipped her arm under Bob's own and led him away, waving at Mesmo.

Eager to pull Bob's attention away from the alien, Laura chit-chatted lightly, pretending not to notice that he was brooding. "Well, that was perfect timing. We were hoping to bump into you."

Bob scoffed. "Bump into me? Or bump into *him*?"

She forced a smiled and squeezed his arm. "There's no need to be jealous."

He didn't answer right away but frowned at the ground while they walked. Then, he stopped and looked at her directly in the eyes. "Listen, baby, I don't want to see you get hurt. I know you'll always see me as the irresponsible teenager I was. But can you believe me when I tell you I have you and Ben's best interest at heart?"

She returned his gaze. She liked this honest side in him. It was a fair question that required a truthful answer. "Of course, Bob. I believe you."

His shoulders relaxed and they continued walking. "It's just that, sometimes I feel like I'm not the only one who's making bad decisions." He glanced at her meaningfully. "Just watch out for yourself, okay?"

Laura avoided his eyes.

What's he getting at, exactly?

She shrugged. "Sure, Bob."

He offered her a smile. "We're bursting with secrets, aren't we?"

Laura returned his smile. "I guess so. Maybe I'll tell you all about them, one day."

They reached the pedestrian crossing.

In a teasing tone, Bob asked, "So, your Mesmo guy is from out of town?"

"Oh yes," she replied casually. "Light years."

CHAPTER 12 *The Lie*

Hao studied Victor Hayward from behind the one-way mirror. The man was slumped on a chair in the interrogation room, his green eyes empty. Only when the police officer sitting opposite him pushed back his chair, did the former businessman jolt, his eyes darting.

The police officer exited the bare room and met Hao on the other side.

"Well?" Hao said.

The officer shook his head. "He's lost it—he's spooked out of his wits. There's nothing to pull out of him."

Hao rotated his body on his crutches and hopped to the door. "I'm expected in the High Inspector's office. Keep me posted if there's any change."

"Yes, Sir."

Hao headed down the plain corridor to the big, metal elevator that would take him to the first floor, which was located just below the surface. As he reached for the elevator button, one of his crutches slipped from his hand and fell with a clatter.

Hao grunted irritably. Man, how he hated these crutches! He couldn't run or defend himself, and everything took double the time to get done.

But I'll get them done—eventually, he promised himself as the elevator rose to his destination.

The doors slid open and he headed for his boss's office. His crutches clicked on the concrete floor, irritating him. He could bet on it that the High Inspector' assistant was watching him struggle all the way to her desk.

He had almost reached her when the office door swung open and Connelly stepped out.

Both men stiffened at the same time.

Connelly closed the door slowly, never taking his eyes off of Hao, then took a few steps in his direction. He pointed at the crutches. "Not planning on using those on me, are you?" he smirked.

Showtime! Hao told himself, but he merely shook his head.

Connelly glared at him for a bit, then said, "You're late. The meeting was moved to 8:00 am. Didn't you get the memo?"

How could I, if no-one sent it to me? Hao fought to keep his inner fire contained. *He's deliberately keeping me out of the loop,* Hao realized. As normal as possible, he answered, "Nope. Must've missed it."

Connelly nodded without smiling. "Well, seeing as you are currently..." he pointed at Hao's broken leg, "...indisposed, High Inspector Tremblay has made it official that I take over the case. I will be answering to him, now."

There you have it! Hao pressed his lips into a fine line. "I see," he said.

The bald man studied him for a bit longer, then passed him by without another word.

"Hey, Theodore!" Hao called after him.

Connelly stopped and turned around.

Hao braced himself, fully expecting to receive a punch in the face. But there was no reaction, so Hao said, "Look, I owe you an apology, you know, for the way I acted the other day in the infirmary. I don't know what got into me." He shuffled on his crutches. "I gotta tell you, I thought I was living my final hours under that avalanche. I even hallucinated. I... I guess fear got the better of me and I took it out on you. It was very unprofessional on my part, and I apologize."

Connelly nodded without a hint of emotion.

Hao wanted to break his nose. "So," he continued instead. "Well done on your raise." He lifted one of the crutches off the ground. "And you're right, of course, it's not like I can do much right now."

Connelly offered him the tiniest of smiles, making Hao's insides twist. Was it a smile of acceptance? A smile of glee? A smile of victory? Hao had no clue.

The men turned their backs to one another after a minimal salute, but then Hao stopped and called after him once more, "Oh, and one last thing."

Connelly cast him a furious look, which Hao thoroughly enjoyed.

"What now?" the bald man snapped.

"Give my best wishes to Kyle."

"To who... *What?*"

Hao frowned. "Today is April second, isn't it?"

"Yeah, so?"

"So," Hao continued. "It's your son's birthday today, isn't it?"

Connelly's eyes narrowed, but only for a fraction of a second.

Jeez, he's good, Hao thought in wonder.

"Right," Connelly said without intonation.

"Sooo," Hao repeated. "Wish him a happy birthday for me when you call him."

Connelly's mouth shut tight, his fingers twitching at his side. He nodded, then spun around and distanced himself from Hao with large strides.

Hao, his brow knitted, bounced unsteadily on his good leg until he had turned a corner. He sagged against the wall and let out a shaky breath. *For goodness sake, the guy doesn't even know his own son's birthday!* Tamara had told him that Kyle's birthday was on April third. Today was April second. And Connelly hadn't known the difference.

Then there was the *Theodore* issue. Connelly hadn't flinched at hearing the name. Whatever was happening, the Connelly he had just spoken to did not match his wife's description of a loving husband and father.

Hao should have felt elated at having caught his partner in a trap, but he didn't. Something was fundamentally wrong, but what was it, exactly?

He only knew one thing for sure—a thing confirmed by the internal alarms that were screaming at him from his entire body. *There's a traitor at the heart of the CSIS.*

* * *

Ben stepped off the bus and waited patiently for the pedestrian light to turn green. As he crossed the street, he was reminded once more that it was the first time he had returned to school without Tike. His heart weighed so heavily he wondered if he was going to be able to carry it.

He had tried hard to concentrate on his first day back at school. Mostly for his mom's sake. It was her first day in a new place as well, after all, and he figured it must be as hard for her as it was for him. So he had put on a brave face.

But attempting to make new friends had been beyond him. He couldn't handle it. Not after having made such great friends in Canmore, only to have them taken away from him at the snap of a finger.

New friendships would have to wait.

He pulled open the door to Uncle Bob's bar. The atmosphere was dim and minimalistic, a bit like Uncle Bob's apartment. It was early afternoon, and the place was empty, except for a person vacuuming at the back and two older folk who stared at him as if he wasn't supposed to be there.

"Hi, Ben!" a cheerful voice greeted him. Pearl appeared from under the counter, her hands full of wet glasses. She placed them on the long counter and headed over to him. "Oh my! Look at you!" she exclaimed, holding him at arm's length to admire him better. "Is that a uniform you're wearing?"

Ben's relief at seeing a friendly face was replaced by fire rising to his cheeks. He nodded.

Not long ago, the prospect of wearing a uniform to school would have unchained a monumental confrontation with his mother. But that was the other Ben, the Ben from before *The Cosmic Fall*. This new Ben hadn't given the grey trousers, white shirt and red tie more than a passing thought. His mind was on other things.

His mind was on Tike who had died, on Mesmo who was on the point of leaving forever, on Beetrix whose species was in danger of dying out... This new Ben was far removed from the trivialities of the clothes he was wearing. That was, unless Pearl mentioned them.

"I'm so glad you're attending school in the neighbourhood and that your mom's decided to help us," Pearl gushed, squeezing his hand, then returning to her position at the counter, where she began to dry a glass with a kitchen towel. "Bobby says you might even settle down in the area."

He thought he glimpsed a tightening under her eyes, but she smiled cheerfully. "We'd love for you to stick around."

Ben nodded again, the theme of where they were going to live a murky question in his mind, then realized he should probably say something. "Thanks. Um, is my mom here?"

"Yes, just head up the stairs to your right. That's the office. Oh, and Ben..." She reached out behind the counter and reemerged with a pile of mail in her hand. "Take these with you, would you? She'll be opening the business mail from now on."

Ben took the envelopes from her.

"And come down when you're done," she added. "I'll teach you to make a mint-orange juice cocktail. You'll see, it's the best in town."

"Okay," Ben said, grinning, then sprinted up the stairs so he could regain control of his burning cheeks. He shoved open the office door, his backpack slipping to his elbow in the process.

He found his mother at a desk with a pile of documents around her.

She placed a pen behind her ear and glued a phone to the other one. She waved at him and signalled for him to wait until she was done. Placing her hand over the speaker, she mouthed, "How was your day?"

Ben gave her a vague thumbs-up. It wasn't as if there was much to say: new buildings, new faces, new teachers. He had waited all day just to be able to join his mother so they could visit Mesmo, for his biggest fear was the alien would take off without saying goodbye.

He dropped his backpack on the floor and rearranged the stack of envelopes from big to small while he waited for Laura to finish her call. Then, he frowned.

Why is the wrong name on the envelopes?

The name printed on them was: ROBERT

MANFIELD.

When Laura hung up, he reached out to give her the mail. "That's weird. Dad's name is on all the enve..." he started, before breaking off. His frown deepened, and he pulled back the mail before she could take it.

Wait a minute... This is really strange...

He studied the envelopes again, completely confused. That was his dad's name, all right, followed by the name of the bar he was standing in, then, its address. "Why is Dad's name on the envelopes?" he asked, but as he spoke, something clicked in the back of his mind, something he should have noticed ages ago, but had been too busy to notice.

"Robert..." he said slowly, his mind whirling. "...and Bob. Aren't those names..." His mouth went dry. He looked up and found his mother's face had turned ashen.

A cold shiver travelled up his spine. "Mom?" he croaked, suddenly engulfed in fear. "Is Bob short for Robert?"

His mother seemed to have turned into a marble statue. No sound came out of her mouth.

Ben stared at her. The envelopes slid, forgotten, from his hands. His brain couldn't believe what he said next. "Mom? Is Bob *my dad*?"

Laura faltered as she got up from her chair. "I need you to listen to me, Ben," she said, hanging on the edge of the desk for support.

Ben's eyes bulged. A simple 'No, honey, don't be silly,' would have done the trick.

Why isn't she answering the question?

"Mom?" his voice rose a pitch. "IS BOB MY DAD?"

Her mouth opened, but nothing came out.

Suddenly, Ben didn't want to hear the answer. He couldn't take it.

"Yes," she said.

Ben flinched as if she had just hit him with a bat.

"There's something you need to understand..." she began, reaching out to him.

Ben recoiled. He couldn't comprehend what was happening. "You mean…. You *lied* to me?" His voice was incredulous.

"I didn't mean to," she whispered, breaking apart before his eyes.

"My dad's alive, and you lied to me ALL THIS TIME?" Memories flashed before his eyes—things that hadn't made sense before, but did now; moments that he should have spent with his dad, but hadn't. Years of lies. He backed into the door.

"No, wait, Ben," Laura said. "Don't turn away from me."

He shook his head in disbelief, then whirled, pulled at the door and bolted down the stairs, ignoring his mother's calls.

"Hey, Ben, are you ready for that orange ju..." Pearl's voice came from behind the counter, but he was already through the door of the pub and out into the bustling street.

He ignored shouts of anger as he bumped into pedestrians. He dashed down the street, zigzagging among afternoon shoppers and office people, putting as much distance as he could between himself and his mother, his heart thudding with each step.

The one person I trusted with my life...

His feet took him to the park, and he kept running even though a stitch nagged at his side. He welcomed the pain. Maybe it would drown his grief. He dropped to the ground at the edge of the lake, sobbing.

Tike! I need you!

He wrapped his arms around his legs and bit into his knee. He shut his eyes tight and screamed into his trouser leg.

Ben rocked back and forth, sobbing his heart out, releasing the pain of Tike's death, trying to make sense of his mother's lie, wondering if he could ever face her or Bob again.

The sun, which reflected a soft orange on the city buildings, did little to warm Ben's insides. He shuddered with thoughts of how his mom had deceived him for years.

A hand touched him on the back. He jumped and laid eyes on Mesmo with relief. The alien sat beside him, and Ben sank his head against his shoulder.

"What happened?" Mesmo asked.

Ben told him.

Mesmo remained silent for a long moment.

When Ben calmed down somewhat, the alien said, "Has your mother told you her reasons? I'm sure there must be an explanation as to why she hid your father from you."

"I don't care. I don't want to hear it."

Mesmo paused, then said, "I've noticed that people sometimes lie to protect their loved ones from painful truths. There is usually a reason behind it. I think you should give her a chance to explain herself."

Ben watched a passing motorboat make ripples on the surface of the lake that slowly trickled to shore, thinking about Mesmo's words. But he felt mentally exhausted and couldn't come up with any reason to listen to his mother. "I want to go with you," he said numbly. "There's nothing left for me here. Grampa, Tike, Kimi, I'll never see any of them again. And now you're going to leave, too." His eyes filled with tears again. "You're the only one left that I can trust."

Mesmo wrung his hands together. "I think you're overreacting right now."

"No, I'm not. I could be your co-pilot. I could learn, you know?" He glanced hopefully at the alien.

Mesmo wrapped his arm around the boy's shoulders and squeezed them without responding. He didn't need to.

Ben's shoulders sagged. "What should I do, then?" he asked, kicking with his heel at the sand.

"Make peace with your mother and father," Mesmo replied. "Bob has offered to help you settle here. You'd be safe here, and you could live close to both your parents. Does that sound so terrible?"

Ben considered it. He had never dared dream of such a thing: to have both a mother and a father in his life. And now it was suddenly a real possibility. But it would be a life without Mesmo. "You stay, then," he shot back. "Teach me how to use the skill! Help me protect the animals! And besides, you love my mom. I saw you kiss her. So, you can't go!"

I sound like a little kid.

"Ben, I..."

"Yes, I know!" Ben interrupted. "The Toreq won't allow you to marry twice or something stupid like that. But you're not on your planet. You're on Earth." He glanced pleadingly at the alien, knowing his reasoning was futile. "What? Does that sound so terrible?" he pressed on anyway.

His words made Mesmo grin. "You are quite a special human being, Benjamin Archer," he said. "And I'm not saying that because of the skill." He fell silent and stared at the lake. When he glanced at Ben again, his smile had faded. "But no, I can't stay."

Ben's head drooped.

"Come," the alien said gently. "I will take you home, to your father. And then I must leave."

They walked side by side through the park, Ben with his hands in his pockets, the red tie of his uniform loose around his neck.

"You know," Mesmo said, "I like it better when you cry from happiness."

Ben smiled sadly and put an arm around the man's waist. "I'm going to miss you," he said.

Mesmo placed his own arm around Ben's shoulders. "I'm going to miss you too, Benjamin Archer."

CHAPTER 13 *Treason*

The elevator to Bob's apartment pinged, and the doors slid open. Ben found his dad pacing beside the kitchen counter with a plastic water bottle in his hand.

"Ben!" he said with some surprise as if he hadn't been expecting him. He stepped forward, but his face fell as soon as Mesmo exited the elevator. Bob licked his lips and drew back.

Ben decided to ignore his father's unwelcome reaction to the alien but felt reluctant to enter the apartment further. His parents' lie loomed like an insurmountable wall before him. "I need to talk to you," he said in a flat voice.

Bob placed the bottle on the counter, then pulled at his collar. "Yes, I need to talk to you, too." His eyes were fixed on Mesmo while avoiding Ben's.

"There's no need. I already know the truth," Ben said glumly. "You're my dad. Mom told me." The words sounded foreign to his ears.

Bob cleared his throat. "I know, she called and told me what happened. She's looking all over for you." He rubbed at the middle of his forehead with his eyes closed. "Look, she made me promise not to say anything. It wasn't supposed to happen this way. We were going to go out, the three of us, have a nice dinner, then talk about it—together. But then, *this* happened." He made a gesture that seemed aimed at Mesmo.

Frustration surged within Ben.

Why's he on Mesmo's back?

Bob's eyes darted across the apartment. He waved the boy over. "Can you come on over here?" he said.

Ben and Mesmo took a step forward.

"Not you," Bob snapped at Mesmo.

Heat flushed through Ben's body. "Will you stop that? Mesmo's my friend. He came to help."

"Just, come on over here, squirt!" Bob demanded irritably, his voice calling for obedience.

Ben approached him, a little apprehensive.

149

He noticed small pearls of sweat on Bob's forehead.

What's up with him?

A reflection on the kitchen fridge moved, making him spin towards the living room. But too late.

From behind a wall, Connelly stepped out with a gun in his hand.

Ben yelped, shrinking into Bob in fright.

"Shh! It's okay! This is a police officer," Bob said, wrapping his arm around the boy's chest.

"No, wait!" Ben shouted, struggling to free himself from Bob's restraining grip.

"Calm down!" Bob urged. "He's here to protect us."

"Are you crazy?"

"Listen to me!" Bob insisted as Ben squirmed. "This Mesmo is a dangerous felon. The police have been chasing him across the country."

"So you went and *called* them?" Ben shouted in disbelief, lunging from Bob's grasp and whirling to face him.

"Relax, will you? I recognized this criminal the minute I laid eyes on him in the park. You can't hang out with people like that! Trust me, I know what I'm talking about. They're dangerous!"

Ben was on the verge of a breakdown. "You

have no idea what you did!" His skin crawled at the shapeshifter's proximity. "He's going to kill us!"

"Don't be stupid. Let the man do his jo..."

Connelly bellowed, "THAT'S ENOUGH!"

Ben whimpered.

The shapeshifter hadn't taken his eyes off Mesmo for a second. His enemy stood near the elevator, poised like a prey backed into a corner.

"This show has gone on long enough," Connelly growled. "Time to wrap up."

To Ben's horror, the bald man aimed the gun at him without taking his eyes off of Mesmo. "Let's go," he said, talking to the boy.

"Wait a minute," Bob protested. "Ben's not going with you. And point that thing elsewhere. Somebody could get hurt."

The bald man turned his head and followed the direction of the gun. Even from where he stood, Ben could see his eyes switching from green to honey-brown. "I won't say it again," he hissed.

Ben knew him well enough to realize that they could all be dead in an instant.

But Bob didn't catch on to the threat. "No, no, Ben has nothing to do with this, I told you already..."

"Get down!" Mesmo yelled.

A blue shockwave lashed out of the shapeshifter, knocking them off their feet. Ben hurled back as if flicked aside by a giant finger. He slammed into the kitchen counter and saw stars before his eyes. Fighting to stay conscious, he found Mesmo sprawled on the floor by the elevator, while Bob lay in a heap beside him. His back throbbing, Ben watched in horror as the shapeshifter's body swelled from internal tremors. He reached for Bob and shook him frantically by the shoulder.

Bob lifted his head dizzily and gasped at the sight unfolding before them.

The shapeshifter groaned and bared his teeth, unable to control his metamorphosis from Connelly into Bordock. An eerie blue light emanated from him as he hunched over, the gun forgotten in his hand.

Ben cast a glance at Mesmo, but the alien lay unmoving.

Bob's eyes, on the other hand, bulged in terror. He scrambled on all fours behind the kitchen counter.

Ben wanted to rush after his dad, but instead, he spotted the water bottle that had been knocked to the ground by the blast and had rolled behind a kitchen stool. He reached for it with the tips of his fingers, then shoved it behind his back in a hurry, checking hastily on Bordock.

The shapeshifter straightened his back, his muscles and bones falling into place. His head spun towards the boy, making a jolt of dread scamper up and down his spine.

Bordock tossed the gun aside. "Useless thing," he said. "Don't make me do that again. Let's go."

Ben cringed and glanced at his dad in a silent plea for help.

But Bob cowered behind the counter, peeking out at the shapeshifter. He waved a trembling hand at Ben, indicating he should obey Bordock at once.

His heart shrinking, Ben stood and carefully side-stepped to where Mesmo lay.

The alien groaned as he regained consciousness. Taking in Ben's fearful eyes and Bordock's glowing hands, Mesmo understood they were helpless. He got up with Ben's help and shoved the boy behind him so he could serve as a buffer.

"Get the elevator," Bordock ordered, his eyes burning with anger.

While Ben obeyed, the shapeshifter

retrieved a police walkie-talkie from within his suit jacket. He pressed a button and spoke into it, "Coming down with the suspects."

Mesmo reacted swifter than lightning.

Ben had placed the water bottle in his hands seconds after helping him up. A rope of water gushed out of the bottle, lashing at Bordock like a whip. It wrapped itself around the shapeshifter, turning into ice instantly.

Caught off guard, Bordock lost his balance and fell heavily.

"Go!" Mesmo yelled to Ben, who was frantically hitting the elevator button. The doors didn't budge.

Mesmo grabbed him by the arm and reached Bob in two long strides. "Is there another way out of here?"

Bob blinked at him and answered with a trembling voice, "Balcony. Emergency stairs."

Mesmo pulled him up roughly. "Take us there, NOW!"

Bob whimpered but did as he was told.

Ben could already hear the ice rope crackling under Bordock's effort to free himself. He stumbled fearfully after Bob. Behind them, the shapeshifter roared.

For the second time, Mesmo yelled, "Down!"

He threw himself on Ben and covered his head with his arms, just as a massive shockwave burst from the shapeshifter. The invisible onslaught hurtled above their heads, crashing into the large windows as if they were made of paper. The glass rippled, then shattered into a thousand pieces that were cast into the air like ice splinters.

* * *

Laura had combed the park searching for Ben and Mesmo and was heading to Bob's apartment when she heard the explosion.

She watched in terror as the windows in Bob's apartment blew outward. Shards of glass flew down into the street like spears, causing havoc that made cars screech to a halt and pedestrians run for cover.

CHAPTER 14 *Shame*

Mesmo urged Ben and his father to their feet.

Bob hopped on to a ledge which led them across the roof of the building. They sprinted to the other side, then clambered down the emergency stairs at the back of the building.

"Hurry!" Mesmo pressed, as if they needed encouragement.

They had almost reached the bottom when Ben risked a look up and felt a chill run down his spine. Bordock was observing them from the rooftop.

They had barely touched the ground when a police car screeched to a stop at the end of the alley. It backed up and turned to head their way.

The three scrambled the other way.

Ben checked over his shoulder. Bordock was still watching them from the rooftop, giving orders into his walkie-talkie. Ben could tell the outline of the alien was changing; he was shapeshifting into Connelly again.

Mesmo rushed them across a street and into another back alley. They hugged the walls when a helicopter flew overhead.

As soon as it was gone, Ben sprinted on, thinking the others were following. But instead, he heard someone groan behind him. He whirled in time to see Mesmo keel over and crash to the ground.

"Mesmo!" he yelled, rushing to his side.

The alien's hands flew to his head.

"What's wrong?" Ben said in anguish, searching frantically for the source of Mesmo's pain.

The alien's body went limp for a fraction of a second, then he came to again with a loud gasp of air.

Whirling sirens zipping by at the end of the alley spurted Ben into action. "Help me!" he urged a pale-faced Bob, while he grabbed Mesmo under one armpit.

Bob's eyes were glazed, but he took Mesmo under the other armpit, and together they dragged the alien into an open warehouse which was filled with piles of boxes.

Although half a dozen men were busy carrying cargo into the back of a store at the end of the warehouse, they found a safe spot in the right corner, behind a wall of boxes and scaffolds covered in plastic.

Ben knelt by Mesmo's side, calling his name, trying to help him regain full consciousness while the alien fought a mysterious, inward battle. It took him almost fifteen minutes to control whatever was happening to him and by the time he blinked his eyes open, his face was grey from the effort.

Ben helped him sit and lean against the boxes. "Are you okay?" he asked, beside himself with worry.

Mesmo nodded, wincing.

"What happened?"

Mesmo had to quiet his rasping breath before he was able to answer. "Spirit portal," he managed to utter.

Ben's eyes fell automatically on his wrist. Then he remembered that the last one to have had the watch with the spirit portal was Mesmo. His mind raced as he realized he hadn't seen it since Mesmo's escape from Victor Hayward's clutches. A sinking feeling filled his stomach. "I don't have it anymore. Do you?"

Mesmo shook his head. "No, but someone tried to impose its effect on me. They tried to force my spirit out of my body. I have never experienced anything so powerful! I barely resisted."

Ben and Mesmo's eyes met. They already knew who it was.

"Bordock!" Ben gasped.

Mesmo nodded. "He is desperate. Not a single Toreq in their right mind would consider doing such a vile thing. Where I come from, forcefully separating a spirit from a physical body is punishable by death. The technology was banned eons ago. Only a handful of Toreq still master that technology." He gritted his teeth. "It can only mean one thing. Bordock is backed by some powerful adversaries."

Ben shuddered at the idea that there could be other Bordocks out there pulling strings, giving the shapeshifter orders.

Mesmo must have seen the fear in Ben's eyes because he placed a hand on the boy's shoulder. "You don't need to worry yourself over that. This is a situation that is taking place on my planet. It does not involve you."

Ben nodded.

"But it also means I need to get home at all costs, to warn my people. Give me a moment to gather my strength," Mesmo said. "Then we need to leave."

Ben nodded again and turned to Bob who was sitting on a box with his face buried in his hands. His pale fingers rubbed at his hair as if the back-and-forth movement kept him from falling into insanity.

"Bob?"

The man stared at the ground. "I didn't sign up for this," Ben heard him say.

"Are you okay?" Ben asked.

His father did not respond.

Ben sighed and turned away, but then he heard Bob say in a clear voice, "You were in the car."

Ben whirled.

Bob hid his eyes in his hands so that Ben could only see his mouth and beard. "Back when you were a baby, and I crashed the car..." He lifted his ruffled head and stared at Ben. "...you were in the car with me," he admitted.

For a second, Ben felt the earth open under his feet, threatening to engulf him. He had to lean against a wall of boxes and slide down to a crouching position to steady himself.

Bob's head was in his hands again. "That's why your mom never forgave me," he said. "I... um... I was really proud of becoming a father. The rest of my friends were too young to be thinking about such things. One afternoon, they got together and insisted I come. So I took you with me to show you off. But I stayed a bit too long, and by the time we headed out again it was dark, and I wasn't thinking straight. That's when I crashed the car."

He stared at the floor. "I panicked. My adult life was just beginning, and I was about to lose everything. I fled and..." His shoulders quaked. "...left you in the car."

Ben listened in disbelief. He tried to process this information, considering the man who was sobbing freely before him. After a while, he reached out and placed a reassuring hand on his dad's leg.

"I was young and stupid," Bob whimpered. "I made a mistake."

Mesmo came up beside Ben. "We have to go," he said softly, but firmly.

Ben forced himself to stand shakily.

His father had his hands to his face again. "I can't do this," he said in a defeated voice.

The boy regarded his father who had the same colour hair and eyes as him. A rebellious mesh stuck out at the back of the man's head, just like Ben, and he knew there was an undeniable blood bond between them.

But Robert Manfield was also numbed by fear, and, although that was a trait Ben knew his mother did not have, he could understand it. How many times had Bordock not had the same effect on him? The difference here was that his dad had a choice to be part of the story, or not. And clearly, he wanted no part of it. Because, whereas Bordock had no interest in his dad, Ben could not say the same. Had Ben been in his dad's position, he probably wouldn't have been up to the task of facing Bordock, either. Few, if any, would accept such a risk. And so, Ben understood.

"Dad," Ben said.

Bob lifted his head.

"I forgive you."

I forgive you for the accident. I forgive you for being too afraid to protect me.

He swallowed a sob.

I forgive you for not wanting to be my dad.

Bob's eyes lit with an inner acceptance of his own weakness. "Then, you are a better man than I ever will be," he said.

Mesmo placed a hand on the boy's shoulder. "Benjamin," he urged. "We can't delay any further."

Ben nodded, reluctant to let go of his father's eyes. "Goodbye, Dad," he whispered as he backed away, but the man had retracted into a shell again.

Boy and alien slipped out of the warehouse, leaving Robert Manfield behind. They sprinted to the end of the back alley, then crouched at the corner to inspect the busy street before them, scanning for police cars.

Ben wiped away the tears that rolled down his cheeks, focusing ahead. He realized they were opposite Berczy Park with its Dog Fountain and wondered if they could make it across without being too obvious.

"Benjamin," Mesmo said, pulling the boy out of his thoughts. Mesmo was observing him curiously.

"What?" he said, sniffing.

"Why did you forgive him?"

Ben stared at the ground, considering the question, trying to ignore a great emptiness growing inside him, and although it hurt, he knew he had done the right thing. He stared at Mesmo and replied, "He made some wrong choices. But at least he tried, and that's good enough for me." He leaned forward again, studying their options, but Mesmo continued to stare at the boy.

Realizing this, Ben frowned. "What is it?"

Mesmo seemed lost in an inner conversation as if he were trying to make up his mind about something. Then he sighed and said, "I think I am beginning to understand something about humans that I didn't understand before."

Ben waited for him to explain himself, but instead, Mesmo said, "You make things very difficult for me, Benjamin Archer."

Ben snorted. "Look who's talking!"

They glanced at each other and grinned.

CHAPTER 15 *Resistance*

Chaos ensued in front of Bob's apartment.

Laura rushed to the scene, her heart thumping, her raincoat flowing behind her as she ran. Police cars halted traffic and surrounded the building entrance. Officers scrambled in and out of the lobby, ambulances whirled to a stop, and first aid crews hurried to check on any injured people who had been unfortunate enough to find themselves under the rain of falling glass.

Laura came to a stop on the other side of the street, desperately trying to figure out what had happened, praying that Ben was not among the wounded.

Then a group of police officers detached themselves from the centre of the commotion and darted down the sidewalk, while a couple of police cars screeched to life, heading the same way. Their sirens wailed down the street.

Laura grasped her handbag tightly. She plunged into the street, oblivious to oncoming traffic, and followed the law enforcement as fast as she could.

* * *

Ben checked the street one more time. "What do you think?" he said.

"We need to keep moving," Mesmo replied.

"There's a bus stop on the other side of the plaza," Ben noted. "We might get lucky. Or we'll come across a taxi."

Mesmo nodded. "Let's go."

They emerged from their hiding spot in the alley and sprinted across the street, forcing a couple of cars to hit their brakes.

They were barely to the other side when the sound of a siren made Ben's blood go cold. He glanced over his shoulder and saw a civilian car bump to a stop on the Berczy Park sidewalk behind him. Two men with bulletproof vests materialized out of the car, one of them barking into a speaker microphone.

"Run!" Mesmo ordered, grabbing him by the back of his shirt collar, almost lifting him up in his hurry to get them going.

Pedestrians froze and looked on in surprise; mothers grabbed their children from the edge of the Dog Fountain and hurried away, while, already, the sound of new sirens approached.

Ben and Mesmo were halfway across the plaza when a helicopter shot over their heads. People shouted and rushed for safety.

"Hold it!" one of the police officers yelled from the civilian car behind them.

"Mesmo!" Ben sobbed, unable to keep up with the alien's long strides. His vision went blurry, and he wiped at his eyes. But the edge of his eyesight began to darken.

What's wrong with me?

"Mesmo!" he called again, his voice sounding far away as if he were crumbling into himself. He couldn't focus or feel the movement of his legs.

Mesmo turned to face him, and Ben vaguely registered the alien's eyes widening in shock. "Benjamin!" he yelled. "Resist!"

Resist what?

That was his last thought before Mesmo's face turned into the granite mosaic paving below him. He did not feel the pain as he hit the ground, however, because already his spirit was plunging through a tunnel of darkness.

* * *

From the opposite side of the street, Laura came to a stop as she watched Ben tumble to the ground. "No!" she yelled in anguish.

Half a dozen police cars rushed to the scene, cutting her off. Two army trucks followed, spewing soldiers, armed to the teeth.

Mesmo stood between Ben and the fountain, frozen in indecision. The soldiers rushed to take position around him, while terrified civilians scrambled in all directions.

Laura looked on in trepidation as the alien hesitated between Ben and his narrowing chance of escape. "Don't leave him!" she begged silently.

Mesmo turned his back on Ben and raced away.

"No!" she breathed, fighting a sudden onset of nausea.

There were yells from the soldiers, who took position to shoot.

In a couple of swift strides, Mesmo's long legs brought him to the fountain. Without pausing, he plunged his glowing hands into the water, and before Laura could open her mouth, a sphere of blue power erupted around the alien, expanding faster than sound towards the soldiers. It was instantly followed by a deafening blast as sound caught up with the expulsed air and an exploding cloud of mist swept across the plaza, knocking over everyone in its path.

Laura toppled as the mixture of air and water shoved her forcefully onto the sidewalk. Shop windows rattled. People lay on the ground, stunned.

Laura picked herself up in a hurry, her head swimming dizzily.

A thick mist emanated from the fountain. The soldiers, who had been hit the hardest, came to their senses and struggled to find their bearings. An eerie silence—only covered by the ringing in Laura's ears and the muffled sound of a helicopter—kept everyone in a daze.

Then people began to scream. They scrambled to their feet, knocking each other over in their haste to escape.

Laura watched dazedly through the running crowds as the mist around the fountain thinned, and Mesmo's outline appeared in its centre. The alien carried Ben in his arms.

* * *

Ben gasped.

He felt as though he had just tumbled down a hill in total darkness and had landed at the bottom, bruised and battered. He figured he must have hit the ground pretty hard and expected pain to engulf him any minute. But the pain didn't come.

Instead, he became aware of muffled silence, cut by screams somewhere far away. He struggled to make sense of sound. His vision focused and he found himself surrounded by metal walls that belonged to the inside of a van. A small window near the front looked out onto an empty driver's seat.

The last thing he remembered was landing face-first on the granite paving. Now, he was in a standing position, inside an unfamiliar vehicle.

How can that be?

He wanted to approach two small, dirt-covered windows on the side of the van but found he couldn't move.

He glanced at his feet and hands, fearfully. There was nothing wrong with them. Yet, when he tried to move, there was resistance. He pressed against the air. An invisible barrier restrained him with force.

Something shone below him. He strained his neck to make out what it was. Blue beams emanated from four hand-sized, black boxes placed in a square formation under his feet. They seemed to determine the limit of his movements.

As if he were stuck in a narrow shaft, Ben managed to bend his knees, grunting as he reached for one of the boxes. He curled his fingers around the object, but his hand passed right through it. Denial seeped into his mind. "No, no, no, no, no." He clung to the word like a life-saving vest.

Unable to fight the horrible, sinking feeling that threatened to engulf him, he stood and stretched his neck to glance out the small windows.

Sounds of screams and running people surrounded the van. He could hear a helicopter hovering overhead. Soldiers gathered before a strange mist which hung to the ground across the street. From it, Ben watched Mesmo emerge, carrying a limp body in his arms.

His body.

"No, no, no, no, no," he repeated. "Mesmo!" He punched at the air that held him prisoner, calling the alien's name desperately. Feeling dizzy with despair, he shut his eyes and puffed his cheeks several times, willing himself to calm down.

Break the connection!

That's what he needed to do.

Take control of your thoughts and break the connection with the spirit portal.

He forced his mind to go blank and willed his spirit back to his body. Instead, a powerful whirlpool of magnetic energy grabbed at him from all sides. He wanted to scream. It was as if he had been swallowed by suffocating quicksand. He didn't know which way was up or down as his spirit stretched in a tug-of-war between his body and the alien trap. Fighting devastating panic, he stopped struggling and let his mind drift. Like a piece of metal drawn to a magnet, his spirit got sucked back into the van.

"Let me out! Help!" he yelled.

Outside the van, chaos drowned his voice.

More police cars arrived at the scene. Ben watched in dismay as his lifeless body was placed on a stretcher and rolled into one of the army trucks. Mesmo was handcuffed and taken into another truck.

The door on the driver's side opened suddenly, and the van dipped as someone took their place in the front seat.

Ben turned in a hurry.

A bald head appeared through the window. "Well, well," Connelly smirked, peeking at him. "I've caught a little mouse." He lifted his arm and tapped on the silver watch that contained the spirit portal. It was safely attached to his wrist. The blue beams below Ben glowed at its proximity.

Ben's voice died in his throat.

Connelly seemed amused. "Don't you just wish I had trapped Mesmo instead of you? His spirit turned out to be too strong, though, and it slipped through my fingers. But then, it occurred to me. Toreq blood now runs through your veins. So, I reactivated my devices and tried again." Connelly clicked his tongue. "I guess my idea paid off."

He turned to face the front, then hesitated and looked back at Ben again, a frown creasing his forehead. "What I didn't expect was Mesmo staying to save you." He shook his head, chuckling. "Or, at least, he made a flimsy attempt to." He raised an eyebrow at Ben's silence. "Lost your voice, little mouse?" He leaned forward and turned on the ignition. The motor roared to life. "Maybe you'll find it again, in the end."

* * *

Laura ran down the sidewalk, bumping into fleeing civilians, trying to approach the group of soldiers who were taking Ben and Mesmo away, while remaining at a safe distance on the opposite side of the street.

A van took off in a cloud of smoke before her, so she stepped onto the parking spot it had left unoccupied. Never once did she take her eyes off Ben's limp body until the back doors of the military truck shut with a clatter, locking him in. The truck sped off without delay, guided by a police car that opened up the way before it, with sirens wailing.

"Ben!" she whispered, weak with worry.

The truck that held Mesmo followed closely behind the first one, and in no time the convoy made their way down central Toronto.

Someone yelled nearby, startling her. A man rushed by, while other people stopped and pointed, commenting loudly. Instead of running away from Berczy Park, she suddenly found civilians heading towards it.

She followed the pointed fingers, and her mouth fell open.

Now that the mist had gone, Dog Fountain

was once more visible in the middle of the plaza. Emerging from its top, a thick column of frozen water sparkled in the afternoon sun. The size of it, in itself, was remarkable, but what caught Laura off guard was the shape the icy cylinder had been twisted into. It was a symbol, and the symbol resembled that of a treble clef—just like the one she had strung around her neck.

CHAPTER 16 *The Interrogation*

Laura wandered the streets of Toronto aimlessly, her mind in turmoil. She clutched the object Mesmo had given her for safekeeping several weeks earlier: the one which he had said contained information.

But what kind of information?

Was the frozen symbol at the fountain meant for her? Did Mesmo expect her to uncover a secret message contained in the gadget somehow?

She slipped into a back alley and crouched against the wall behind some garbage bins, then pulled out the object and studied it up close. It was the length of her pinkie and was made from a heavy material. She noted once more that it vaguely resembled the musical symbol commonly placed at the beginning of music partitions. There were tiny indentations and bumps along the surface, but nothing giving the slightest hint as to how it functioned.

Laura leaned back and let out a shaky breath. *What now?*

A racket down the alley made her start. She peeked out of her hiding spot behind the garbage bin and saw a form hunch out the garage doors of a warehouse, pushing aside empty boxes that stood in his way. She tensed, preparing to flee. But the man headed in the opposite direction without noticing her.

Is that...?

"Bob?" She got to her feet instantly. "Wait up!"

The bearded man glanced at her, then hastened away.

"Hey!" she yelled, sprinting after him.

Bob broke into a run, but not fast enough that she couldn't catch up with him.

"Stop already!" she panted, grabbing his arm. "Why are you running?" She fell back at the sight of his harried look.

He cringed at her touch.

"What's the matter?"

His eyes darted from side to side. "Danger," he muttered. "Have to go…"

"Wait a minute! What happened? Tell me!"

He wouldn't meet her eyes. "This police officer came to my condo… I thought he was… but his face! His face… Not normal…"

"I know about him already. The police just took Ben away. He's in grave danger! We have to do something!"

Bob rocked on his feet without looking at her.

"Bob!" she yelled, trying to shake him into action. "Come on! We have to save Ben!"

Ben's father remained silent.

Laura lifted her arms in surrender and backed away from him.

Bob scrubbed at his face with his hands. "I… this is not… You never said…"

Laura pressed her hands against her stomach. "I get it," she nodded slowly. "You're doing it again! You're running away!"

Bob dropped his chin to his chest as if she had just slapped him in the face. "No! I… I need to think… I… we could get killed… This is too dangerous… Need to hide…"

She watched him mutter as he distanced himself from her, feeling too numb to retain him.

She so needed Bob's help right now, but clearly, Bordock had left a lasting mark on him. Could she blame him?

I'm terrified of Bordock, too.

But turning her back on Ben was out of the question. And with that in mind, she realized there was only one thing left for her to do.

* * *

Connelly drove further and further away from any signs of civilization, with Ben catching glimpses through the small dust-covered windows of the traffic-jammed Toronto streets to hills covered in maple trees that went on and on for as far as the eye could see. Darkness fell, making the whole trip even lonelier.

Where's he taking me?

The longer the drive, the more desperate he became, especially after the van veered on to a bumpy road, away from the main, asphalted highway.

This spirit travelling didn't sit well with him. He yearned to return to the real, physical world and be in charge of his movements. The invisible pressure exerted all around him made it hard for him to concentrate. It was as if an elephant sat on him, making it necessary to focus his every thought on not getting crushed.

Now I know how Mesmo felt all these months.

The van finally came to a stop many hours later, in the pitch of the night. Ben briefly caught sight of a convoy of trucks and soldiers bustling around an open area illuminated by LED floodlights, in the middle of which stood a dull, concrete building.

The van, however, came to a standstill under the shadow of trees, far enough away not to be noticed.

Connelly turned to him. "Don't try anything funny," he warned, before getting out and shutting the door.

The shapeshifter's footsteps faded away, leaving Ben in a crushing silence.

How am I going to get out of this one?

* * *

The heavy Dugout elevator came to a standstill. Three soldiers stepped out of it, flanking the tall alien that Hao had been searching for for a good six months. The Inspector watched, along with a dozen other bystanders, as the subject strode across the hangar dominated by the hovering spacecraft.

Just look at him, Hao thought, observing the man's traits: wavy, brown hair, high cheekbones, square chin and straight nose. Slightly taller than the average male. Nothing out of the ordinary. *He dyed his hair,* Hao realized suddenly.

He followed the apprehended suspect across the hangar, briefly noticing that he was getting used to his crutches. But while the soldiers took the alien to the interrogation room, Hao split from the group and headed down to the last floor.

There, he found men in protective suits rushing around the safe room containing the three lifeless aliens, and Hao watched as the boy was rolled on a stretcher beside the alien girl.

The medical team shouted orders to each other and Hao had to wobble aside as a heart monitor and other medical equipment were rushed to the boy's side.

"What's going on?" Hao asked sharply, addressing a passing medic. "Is he alive?"

The practitioner lifted his surgical mask. "Barely," he said, wiping his brow with the back of his arm. "His heart rate is dangerously low. Zero reflex responses. We're treating it as a coma."

Hao pressed his lips together.

The practitioner covered his mouth again and adjusted his latex gloves. "It would help if we knew what happened to him. You could consider slipping the question to his alien accomplice." Without waiting for a response, the practitioner went to join the rest of the medical team.

Hao backed away with dullness in the chest. He did not like it when an investigation went awry. In his mind, if anyone got hurt—be it police, civilian or suspect—it meant unprofessional coordination of the special forces. A successful intervention should occur in a quasi-invisible and swift manner, with as little disturbance to civilians as possible. Hao exhaled air out of his puffed cheeks.

This case is one mess after another, he thought scornfully.

He clambered back up the stairs and headed for the interrogation room. The soldier standing guard moved aside sharply.

Good, Hao thought. *This one still thinks I'm in charge.*

He entered the dark room and observed the alien sitting behind the one-way mirror. A soldier stood guard beside the subject, while another flanked the wall beside Hao.

"Where's Agent Connelly?" Hao asked the

guard.

"He's debriefing the High Inspector, Sir," the guard replied. "They'll be down in a minute."

Good. Out loud, Hao said, "Well, I don't have all day. Open up, will you?"

"But Agent Co..."

"...will be down in a minute, you just said. I'm to begin questioning the suspect at once."

The guard shifted, but Hao knew he still exerted enough authority to be obeyed.

Might as well use it while it lasts, he thought bitterly.

"Yes, Sir." The guard straightened and hurried to unlock the door with a code. It buzzed open, and Hao stepped in.

"I'd like to speak to the suspect, alone," he told the guard who stuck by the wall like a poster.

"That is not advisable, S..." the guard began.

"*I'll* determine what *is* and what *isn't* advisable, soldier. You will leave me with the suspect!"

The soldier knocked his army boots together. "Yes, Sir!" He exited the room with quick strides, and the door clicked heavily shut behind him.

Hao paced the room, his crutches clicking on the floor.

The subject sat with his eyes closed, his skin a light shade of grey, his cuffed hands resting on the table before him.

Hao couldn't help but stare in fascination at the extraterrestrial. Had this individual really crashed in one of the alien spaceships that they had recovered on the fields of Chilliwack? Up until this moment, Hao had felt like he had been chasing a phantom. Months of research had only revealed fleeting glimpses of the subject: a lousy image from an airport camera, a grainy picture from a funeral, and a glance of the man fleeing on the Kananaskis Mountains...

Placed next to the other deceased aliens, there was an undeniable similarity. And then there were the hundreds of questions he had about inexplicable whale and crow attacks, the fact that this individual had survived a massive avalanche unscathed, and the many news reports that were surging of the Berczy Park incident with a mysterious, frozen symbol perched on top of its fountain.

Not to mention that there's no trace of him in any official identification system.

Even though he did not have a shred of hard evidence to link this individual to *The Cosmic Fall*, his gut feeling told him that the right suspect had been apprehended—meaning he was once more in the presence of an extraterrestrial being. Hao's stomach felt queasy.

How does one initiate a conversation with an alien? he wondered.

Hao wished he had time to ask the millions of questions that crisscrossed his mind, but they would have to wait. He sat opposite the suspect and said, "My name is Inspector James Hao. My partner, Agent Theodore Connelly, will be joining us soon."

The alien opened his eyes. They were a deep honey-colour. They reflected extreme weariness, yet Hao's heightened senses also perceived the hint of a connection between them.

"How is the boy?" the subject asked.

Hao had hoped for a mutual introduction, but clearly, the alien was testing the ground on which he stood. "Benjamin Archer, you mean?" he replied, deciding to go along with the alien's side of the conversation. "We believe he is in a coma. You can rest assured that he is being closely monitored by our medical team."

The alien gave a single nod.

"Can you tell me what happened to him, so our doctors can treat him, accordingly?" Hao asked.

The alien studied him as if trying to determine how much he should say. "Perhaps you should ask that question to the one you call your partner," he replied finally.

Hao flinched involuntarily. "Why?"

The alien held his gaze with a glint in his eyes but did not answer.

There's that connection again. "What would my partner know, that I don't?" Hao insisted. It bothered him that the subject didn't look away once. *He wants to talk but is cautious.*

Voices came from the other side of the one-way mirror.

Damn! "Talk to me!" Hao urged. "What would my partner know about the boy that I don't? I already know he's not human. My partner took a blood sample from him."

The alien leaned forward, his eyes glued to Hao, and spoke in a low voice, "Did he, really?"

Hao opened his mouth, but just then lights came on in the adjacent room, making the High Inspector and Connelly visible through the smoked glass.

Connelly approached the window to glance at them, then lifted his arm and tapped on his silver wristwatch meaningfully, as if indicating that Hao's time was up.

The door swung open, and the High Inspector stepped in, eyes protruding. "Hao, what do you think you're doing?"

Hao didn't have time to reply.

The alien's reaction was swift. He sprang out of his chair, shoved the High Inspector aside and threw himself at Connelly. The bald man toppled under the attacker's weight.

Chaotic shouts broke out. The two guards rushed to Connelly's aid and tore the alien away from him, then dragged the suspect back into the interrogation room, pinning him down on the chair. The High Inspector and Connelly picked themselves up from the ground, shakily.

Hao gaped from the alien to his colleagues. He grabbed his crutches and hopped out of the room. "Do you have that effect on everyone?" he taunted his partner.

Connelly glowered at him while he straightened his jacket and wiped at the dust on his arms.

Hao turned to his boss. "I take it you don't require my assistance for this interrogation?"

The High Inspector yelled, "Get out of here! I'll deal with you later."

"Yesss, Sssir!"

Just before the door to the interrogation

room shut behind him, Hao took due note of the furious stare that the alien was directing at Connelly. *What's up with him?* he wondered.

He stepped into the hangar where he contemplated the spacecraft without really seeing it. *Connelly,* he thought. *Everything always leads back to Connelly.*

His mind whirled. He had told the alien that Connelly had taken a blood sample from the boy and he had replied, "Did he, really?" Why had he said that? And why had the alien attacked Connelly specifically instead of himself, too? Clearly, something was going on between his partner and the suspect. If only he could figure out what it was.

"Inspector?" A woman with a grey skirt and white shirt ran up to him, pulling him out of his thoughts. "Have you seen Agent Connelly?"

Man, our wonder boy truly has made himself indispensable around here, Hao seethed. The Inspector leaned on one of his crutches and pointed behind him. "He's busy right now."

"Oh," the woman said, her shoulders dropping.

"What is it?"

"I have a phone call for him. It's that woman, Laura Archer? She says she wants to turn herself in."

CHAPTER 17 *Fireworks*

What's happening out there?

Not knowing threatened to plunge Ben into an uncontrollable panic. He felt as though he were on the edge of a black hole, looking down. The swirling quicksand inside the hole reached its sticky fingers around his spirit, intent on tearing it apart as it tried to return to his physical body. He dare not try anything for fear he would tip over into the void.

How did Mesmo do it?

How had the alien managed to fight off the spirit portal's powerful tug? He closed his eyes and embraced the despair that swept through his mind.

No hope...

Benjamin Archer?

Something whispered faintly in his ear.

I'm going crazy, he thought.

There was a sound like rushing water, and from somewhere far away, he heard his name being called. He opened his eyes again and felt warmth emanating from his hands. They glowed a transparent blue.

Benjamin Archer?

Beetrix?

He held still with expectation.

Benjamin Archer? Where are you?

Beetrix! His mind burst with relief.

Beetrix buzzed at the edge of his thoughts.

I feared the worst. Your body lies immobile, yet I sensed your presence. How can that be?

I am trapped in the van. Please help me!

The bee's thoughts strengthened in his mind.

You may come.

Ben's eyes rolled back into his head, and suddenly he was floating outside the vehicle, looking back at it. He felt a cool breeze on Beetrix' wings, and leaves from the maple trees swayed above him.

I'm free!

For a split second his mind leapt with

elation. But Beetrix' words crushed his hopes.

I feel your spirit weakening. I fear for your life.

Ben felt Bordock's trap tug at him, exerting pressure from all sides. He hadn't been miraculously freed at all.

I'm only using the translation skill.

Mesmo's words echoed in his mind: *The skill is not connected to the body. It is connected to the spirit.* Meaning Beetrix was providing him with a window to the outside, but his situation had not changed.

Beetrix' thoughts reached him.

What is happening, Benjamin Archer! I sense great danger...

But Ben wasn't listening. He had barely connected with Beetrix when he spotted the shapeshifter reach the van, open its back doors and disappear inside. Overcome with panic, he gagged as he disconnected with the queen bee and his thoughts tumbled back into the vehicle. When his sight adjusted, it was to come face to face with Connelly.

"What are you doing?" the shapeshifter growled.

"N-nothing," Ben gasped, wishing he could be anywhere else but here. Beetrix fluttered at the boundary of his mind. He shut her out entirely so his hands wouldn't glow.

Connelly eyed him suspiciously, his irises switching from green to honey-brown.

Ben noted that the shapeshifter was not in a good mood.

"I don't trust you," the bald man said. "Don't try anything funny while I go deal with your Toreq friend."

Fear gripped Ben's mind. "Where's Mesmo? What have you done to him?" he blurted.

Connelly bent on one knee to check on the black boxes. "You can forget about that scum. His hours are counted."

Ben felt the space around him tighten. "Why are you doing this?" he gasped.

The shapeshifter straightened and set cool eyes on him. "There will be time, later, to discuss the reasons for my actions."

Ben's stomach twisted. *I don't want to be here, later.*

He thought frantically. "Killing Mesmo won't change anything. Just leave us alone. What does it matter to you? Once you leave with your spaceship, Mesmo won't be able to follow. Don't you see? Whoever is waiting for you up there won't know the difference."

Connelly cast him a dark look that made him cringe. "*I'll* know the difference," he said. "His remains will be proof that I accomplished my task."

"Proof? For who? I bet even the A'hmun you work for wouldn't accept such foul actions..."

Ben thought he saw a sly smile creep onto the shapeshifter's face.

"Who said anything about working for the A'hmun?"

"What? But you..."

"Enough!" Connelly snapped. "Don't try to delay me any further." He hopped out of the van. His teeth reflected the cold floodlights, and before slamming the doors, he said, "Watch for fireworks."

* * *

Connelly stepped out of the elevator on the bottom floor of the Dugout and smiled. His spacecraft hovered before him, sleek and black, waiting for him. He had longed for this moment for so long. Finally, the pieces of the puzzle were falling into place. Not only would he get rid of Mesmo and his team, but he would return to the Mother Planet with a coveted prize: the translation skill.

These months of hardship, posing as Agent Connelly, had paid off, and he was going to enjoy every moment of the coming hours.

But first, he had to clear the area so he could operate undisturbed. He glanced up at the concrete ceiling, conscious that his means of transport was buried deep under the ground of the Dugout. The several floors built above his spaceship did not worry him, however.

He walked to his vessel, savouring every moment of his imminent victory while soldiers and men in lab coats went about their business around the hangar. He reached for the spacecraft's smooth surface, his fingers tingling with anticipation, and instantly the door mechanism obeyed his touch, sliding open to reveal the inside.

As he hopped on board, he caught sight of a couple of men in lab suits stopping in their tracks, their eyes popping out of their heads.

Connelly chuckled. "Better scamper, cockroaches," he muttered as he closed the door behind him.

He immersed himself in a regenerative light, recovering his normal traits through waves of pain imposed by his shapeshifting skill.

As soon as he was done, he slipped into the

pilot seat, cleared the front window, and began activating the vessel, taking no notice of the cries of alarm from stunned men who gathered in the hangar. The spacecraft vibrated with a low, constant buzz, indicating that an inner mechanism had been brought to life.

Bordock swiped at screens and symbols that materialized before him. The spacecraft huffed and emitted a low, repetitive hum.

The shapeshifter skimmed over symbols that scrolled down in mid-air to make the constant throbs more pronounced. Bluish light left the craft and washed over the hangar, each vibration causing the walls to ripple. Men yelled and scrambled in all directions, their hands pressing against their ears as sirens blared and concrete wall cracked.

Thick slabs detached from the floor above, then crashed to the floor of the hangar, sending soldiers dashing for the stairs like miniature ants.

The blue shockwaves turned orange, then red, rising in intensity, causing destruction as soon as they hit anything in their path. Thick slabs fell from above, some landing with a deep thud on the craft, but Bordock only smiled and increased the destructive power.

One after another, the consecutive floors

that imprisoned the spacecraft from above came crashing down on the hangar floor.

* * *

The taxi came to a stop next to a back alley. Hao checked the shadows for signs of life, then, seeing none, paid the taxi driver and clambered out of the vehicle. The driver sped off into the night, leaving Hao on his own.

He checked the time on his phone. It was one o'clock in the morning. Eight hours had passed since the alien had been arrested not far from this Toronto street; three hours since Laura Archer had contacted him and told him to meet her here.

Good thing the High Inspector hadn't confiscated his CSIS badge, yet. Hao had taken a helicopter from the Dugout to Toronto in no time. He needed answers, and he needed them soon before Connelly managed to find a way to kick him out of the Intelligence Services altogether.

Hao tightened his grip on his crutches and made his way down the dark alley, realizing he could very well be walking into a trap with no means to defend himself.

Large garage doors opened onto a dark warehouse filled with boxes. Hao stepped in and placed himself in the centre of the storage place to be visible. His phone buzzed in his inside pocket. He silenced it without even glancing at the screen, focused on scanning the darkness. "Laura Archer!" he called. "I'm Inspector James Hao with the CSIS."

A gust of wind swirled into the warehouse, lifting dust and rippling sheets of plastic that covered scaffolds in the back.

"Ms. Archer?" he repeated.

Only silence greeted him, and for a minute Hao figured he had lost a precious three hours.

He clicked impatiently with the crutches on the ground when a woman's voice spoke from the gloom. "Where are the others?"

Hao squinted and thought he saw a shadow standing by the scaffolds. "What others?"

"I'm turning myself in. Where's your backup?"

Yes, the woman was standing behind the sheets of plastic, Hao confirmed. He shifted to face her better. "It's just me," he said.

Her form cut out against the gloom and stepped towards the exit.

"Wait!" Hao called, realizing she could make

a run for it. "I'm unarmed."

The woman slowed down. "I don't trust you," she said.

"Look at me," Hao urged. "My leg's broken. I'm on crutches, for goodness sake! It's not like I can catch up with you."

She studied him from a safe distance. "I turned myself in to be with Ben," she said, then backed away. "I'll find another way."

"Hold on!" Hao called after her. "I understand that you don't trust me. But I came on my own because I need to talk to you about my partner, Agent Connelly."

This made Laura Archer pause.

She knows something! he realized.

Out loud, he said, "I need to understand what's going on. I need you to tell me what you know, one-on-one." Because she seemed to hesitate, he added, "Talk to me, and then I promise I'll take you to see the boy."

Her voice trembled. "Is he alive?"

"He is, but he slipped into a coma."

He heard her sob.

"He's being treated by our best doctors, Ms. Archer, you can count on it," he added quickly.

She stepped forward, a service light illuminating her face. "All right. Stay where you are," she said. "What do you want to know?"

"First off, tell me about Benjamin Archer."

"What about him? He's my son."

"We have his blood sample. It's like nothing we have ever seen before. It's not... human."

She approached him slowly and regarded him with cold eyes. "And that blood sample, who took it?"

"My partner, Agent Co..." Hao broke off, and then it hit him.

She watched his reaction and nodded. "That blood sample didn't come from my son," she said. "Your partner extracted it from himself."

Hao's mouth went dry. The past months flashed before his eyes.

She stood before him now. "The one who calls himself Agent Connelly is not who he says he is. His real name is Bordock. Bordock killed the real Agent Connelly on the night of *The Cosmic Fall* and took on his appearance. He is a shapeshifter."

Hao felt the blood drain from his face. "An alien...?"

Laura nodded.

Hao staggered back a few steps and plopped down on a box. "Agent Connelly..." he whispered, thinking back. "...was the first to arrive at the crash site..."

"Yes, the real Agent Connelly is among Bordock's growing list of victims. You see, Bordock shot down the spaceships that crashed on the night of *The Cosmic Fall*. Only one occupant survived, and Bordock wants him dead. That's why he took on the form of a police officer to infiltrate the CSIS. He's been using your organization to track down his enemy."

"Your alien friend?"

Laura nodded again. "Yes. His name is Mesmo." She bent on one knee to be level with him, eyes pleading. "Please, you've got to help me. Mesmo and Ben are at Bordock's mercy right now. You've got to take me to them."

Hao rubbed a hand over his face, thinking about what she had said. As crazy as the whole thing sounded, her explanation joined the pieces of the puzzle that were scattered in his mind. He had seen some unbelievable things in the past weeks, but this one topped all of them. Had he really been duped? Connelly's face hovered before his eyes. Instinct told him she was telling the truth, and so he decided to believe her.

"I've been going about this all wrong, haven't I?" he said, half to himself. He tugged at his bottom lip, going over the different events of the past months.

Laura cast him a look of sympathy. "It's not your fault. Bordock had us all fooled."

Yes, but I trained years for this. I should have seen it long ago. Hao cast her a sombre look, trying to process the information. "Don't get me wrong, Ms. Archer. I was only doing my job. I needed to determine whether *The Cosmic Fall* posed any threat to our people, our nation, possibly even to our world. You and your son's constant evasion of the law was highly suspicious."

"We had no choice but to run," she said. "Bordock—your partner—wants to see us dead, too, even though the enmity between Bordock and Mesmo has nothing to do with us. Mesmo is no threat. He just wants to get home alive..."

"But what are they doing here? Are they planning an invasion?" Hao burst out.

To his surprise, Laura gave him a wry smile.

"I asked Mesmo the same thing, not long ago," she said. "But no, his people are no danger to us. He says small teams visit Earth at regular intervals. They do that all over the universe, to observe and gather knowledge, but nothing else."

"What about this shapeshifter? Why would he want to see you dead?"

Laura became even more restrained. "We've

been helping Mesmo since he arrived. I guess that hasn't been to Bordock's liking."

"...and yet," Hao pointed out, "It is this Bordock—the very man you have been trying to avoid—that you tried to contact at the CSIS to turn yourself in..."

Laura cast her eyes down. "I figured he'd take me to Ben." She interlaced her fingers and sobbed. "I didn't know what else to do."

Hao stared at her in stunned silence. *She's willing to risk her life to be with her boy...*

His phone buzzed. He reached for it, but just then the sound of a roaring engine filled the warehouse. A black van screeched to a stop in the middle of the exit, its front lights blinding them. Side doors flew open and half a dozen men rushed towards them, threateningly.

"Watch out!" Hao yelled, shoving Laura behind him.

One of the men charged him. He barely had time to react, when the sharp contact of the man's knuckles on his chin knocked him over. Everything went dark.

CHAPTER 18 *The Last Key*

Ben sensed, more than felt, the vibrations that began to shake the ground.

He didn't register them right away because the pressure coming from the four black boxes had become unbearable. His spirit was squeezed too tight, his thoughts scrambled. He knew Beetrix was calling him from somewhere far away, but he couldn't concentrate on connecting with her with all his energy going into surviving the suffocating quicksand that pressed on him from all sides.

The van lurched loudly. His eyes flew open. Through the side windows of the van, Ben caught sight of shadows of running soldiers stretched before the LED floodlights. The vehicle trembled.

What's going on?

His mind felt as though he were suffering from a fever, where everything becomes distorted. The van lurched again, and a rumbling sound came from deep within the ground. Then again. And again.

Ben gasped.

A LED flood light teetered and crashed, the earth shook as if a superhuman being was hitting it repeatedly with a giant hammer, and to his horror, Ben watched as the concrete building crumbled in on itself and disappeared.

Ben yelled, willing the destruction to stop.

When the earthquakes died down, the rattling walls of the van settled, and the night reclaimed its silence.

A branch thudded onto the roof of the van, making Ben yelp. He strained his neck to glance through the windows. Where once there had been an open area surrounded by trees, now red steam swirled out of a deep wound in the ground resembling the mouth of a seething volcano.

Ben's mind spun with one terrifying thought:

The spacecraft is free to leave!

* * *

"Inspector!" Laura's voice came out hushed but frantic, because the bound man lay unresponsive beside her.

"Inspector!"

"It's James, actually," Hao groaned, moving his bruised jaw from side to side. He blinked and forced himself to a sitting position.

Relief washed over her and she realized this government agent had suddenly turned into an ally. "Are you all right?" she whispered, glancing anxiously at the four thugs who stood behind them, waiting. *Waiting, for what?*

Hao opened his mouth to answer, but a persistent sound distracted them. The Inspector's phone lay on top of a pile of boxes five feet away, humming endlessly.

Too far, Laura thought.

Two guards lowered a wheelchair from the van, its headlights bathing them in such a bright light that Laura had to squint. The wheelchair rolled easily toward them, the driver manoeuvring it with a simple handswitch.

The person stopped before them and turned so that the headlights illuminated his face.

To Laura's surprise, it was an old man. He sported a white goatee and his longish grey-white hair was gathered in a short ponytail at the back of his head. His slanted eyes observed them without a hint of emotion. He waved a hand with long, knobbled fingers at the phone.

In the blink of an eye, one of his men cut the call, then stood on guard once more.

When no-one moved, Hao spoke. "I work for the federal secret services. Whatever this is about, you should be dealing with me. Let the woman go."

The old man ignored him and said something Laura understood to be Chinese.

In response, one of the guards grabbed Laura by the arm, making her yell.

"Wait! What are you doing?" Hao shouted.

The guard pulled at something around Laura's neck and it snapped.

The necklace!

"That's mine! Give it back!"

The guard held up the necklace to the old man, who studied it with interest. He spoke slowly, searching for English words. "You must forgive the rough treatment." He gave an order to his men who acted at once.

Laura felt the bonds slip from her wrists.

Hao glanced questioningly at Laura, as he was also freed.

"My name is Su Tai," the old man said. "We

had to be sure it was you. We mean you no harm."

Laura saw Hao glare at the guard who had punched him in the chin and got a cold look in return. "If you mean us no harm, then free the woman," Hao insisted.

"All in good time," Su Tai said. "It is she I have come to talk to."

Laura tensed.

The phone hummed again.

The old man glanced at it, unfazed. "There isn't much time." He turned his attention to Laura. "The Observer has sent us an urgent message. You have been of invaluable assistance to him so far, and you have put yourself in great danger. Yet, I must ask you to continue to do so, for the Observer's mission is at stake."

"What message?" Hao whispered to Laura.

Laura's eyes widened. "The fountain!" she exclaimed to the old man. "You saw the symbol Mesmo created on the fountain!"

Su Tai smiled. He held the small, black object in the palm of his hands. "I came at once and searched for you. But it is the Inspector who led me to you."

Hao twitched beside her, and she was sure he was bursting with questions like she was.

But the old man continued. "The Observer

has entrusted you with Angakkuq's life's work."

Angakkuq.

Laura's mind reeled. That was the mysterious woman who had given Mesmo the symbol back in Canmore.

One of the guards approached Su Tai with a box, which he opened. The old man pulled something small from it and placed it in his palm. He now had two identical objects in his hand.

Laura gasped.

"It is highly irregular to trust an outsider with such sensitive information, but the Observer has spoken well of you and, considering the precarious situation in which he now finds himself, I have no choice but to hand over my life's work to you as well."

A guard picked up both objects from Su Tai's palm. He brought them over and placed them in Laura's hands as if they were breakable crystals.

"Laura Archer," Su Tai said. "The Observer never made it to China to meet with me. I have travelled a long way so he could receive this last element. Should you succeed in bringing them both to him, then he will return home a hero, his mission fulfilled."

Laura gaped. "You are one of the Wise

Ones!" Mesmo's words flooded her mind: *"I came to assess the planet. My people have been doing so since before the beginning of the Human era, every two hundred Earth years. Seven Wise Ones report to us from different parts of the planet, from places you currently call Bolivia, Australia, Kenya, Polynesia, Norway, China and Northern Canada. I have met with six of them now. My last stop after Bolivia was going to be China, but then I came back here instead and was waylaid..."*

Laura blinked and focused on the old man. He smiled at her and nodded.

"And you..." Su Tai said, turning his attention to Hao. "...you have the access Laura Archer needs to reach the Observer. So, I will ask you, as one compatriot to another, to bring Laura Archer to the Dugout and protect her from the corrupt shapeshifter."

"What?" Hao gasped. "How do you know about the Dugout?"

The old man gestured towards the buzzing phone. "We have eyes and ears everywhere, Inspector James Hao. You have served your organization well, but have made the wrong choices. From now on, you will protect the Observer, the woman, and the boy."

"Is that so?" Hao retorted. "Who do you

think you are? I do not serve you. And I am not your compatriot."

"You are right," Su Tai said. "That was a bad choice of words. While we may have come from the same region of this planet, current borders have no meaning to our situation. Those I serve transcend human history. I am here merely to assist the Observer."

Laura burst into the conversation. "You are Toreq?"

Su Tai smiled at her. "Do not mistake the colour of my hair for that of the Toreq. No, I am of A'hmun descent, though I do serve the Toreq. I have served them well. I had hoped that the Observer would concede me a one-way ticket back to the Mother Planet." His smile faded. "But that is no longer to be."

The light on Hao's phone came on, indicating a new incoming call.

"Our shapeshifter is up to something," the old man said, his face becoming gloomy as he glanced at the phone. "You must hurry." He turned his wheelchair around and rolled away from the pair. "I am counting on you, Inspector. And on you, Laura. Forgive me for imposing this burden on you both, but I know that, together, you can free the Observer and send him home.

He has already lost his life companion and his daughter, he does not deserve further wrath from the shapeshifter." Su Tai was almost halfway to the van.

The other guards blended into the shadows after him. As they lifted the wheelchair, Laura heard him say, "And if you succeed, I trust he will speak a good word for you, when the time comes."

The van doors rolled shut. The motor roared to life, and the vehicle sped away.

Hao hopped to the pile of boxes and grabbed his ringing phone, pressing the call button.

Even from her seated position, Laura could hear a man's screaming voice erupt out of it.

"Sir! Where are you? The Dugout is under attack! I repeat, we are under attack!"

CHAPTER 19 *Waking Dragon*

The helicopter landed on a bustling airfield. Hao leaned on Laura's shoulder to clamber out of it. Her hair whipped his face as the rotors continued to turn.

A military jeep stood a few feet away, a soldier ready to lead them into action. LED floodlights illuminated the airstrip, and army trucks passed marching soldiers at high speed.

Hao and Laura took places in the jeep, heading for the source of the commotion. They reached a fence topped with barbed wire and had to come to a halt to avoid running into an armed guard.

"Back away!" the man ordered.

Hao waved his badge. "Inspector Hao. I have clearance."

Laura grabbed his shoulder. He turned to find her leaning forward, staring ahead.

Hao did the same and felt a cold ripple travel up and down his back.

Before them, trees burned and men and women scrambled for safety. Some of them were visibly hurt. But what made Hao's blood turn cold, was an eerie red mist that escaped from an enormous, gaping hole where the Dugout had once been. Hao dropped back into his seat and yelled to the driver, "You! Get out!"

The soldier glanced at him with wide eyes, then hopped out of the vehicle.

"Laura!" Hao barked. "Take the wheel!"

Laura slipped into the driver's seat, pressed the gas pedal and bypassed the guard who was shouting at them to stop.

Hao grasped the side of the car, half to avoid painful jolts to his leg, half from increasing dread as to what they would find ahead.

Laura hit the brakes near the hole. They stepped out, hypnotized by the crater that looked like the mouth of a volcano.

"Ben!" she breathed, breaking into a run.

"Hey!" Hao scrambled to catch up with her and grab her arm just as she was about to loose her footing in her haste to glance over the edge.

Wisps of red, hot water vapour lifted from a dark mass that lay at the bottom, resembling a waking dragon.

Hao and Laura stared at each other as if to give each other strength.

"Ben's down there," she said, eyes pleading.

"This way," he said, ignoring his thumping heart. He had spotted a set of stairs on the outskirt of the hole to their left—only, it was one floor down, and there was no way to get to it.

We'll have to jump, he realized.

Laura glanced at him and drew her eyebrows together.

"I can make it," Hao reassured her.

She nodded and headed to the edge of the hole. Hao watched as she grabbed on to the side, then swung down. He heard a muffled thud and peeked down hurriedly.

Her voice sounded distant. "It's okay," she shouted. "The landing is clear, but you risk falling on your injured leg."

Hao didn't wait to hear more. He dropped his crutches and heard them clatter next to Laura. Sitting on the edge, he lowered himself over the side, copying Laura, then hung on until he had determined how far down the floor was.

"Careful!" Laura warned.

He let himself drop, landing on his good leg, but lost his balance and tumbled into Laura as she tried to break his fall. They landed in a heap on the floor, Hao's broken leg bumping on the concrete. "Ouch!" he yelled, biting back a harsher word.

"Are you okay?" Laura gasped.

Hao shut his eyes. "Never better," he groaned, drawing in a sharp breath. *Damn, this is going to hurt.* He bit his tongue and accepted Laura's help as they stood. She passed him his crutches.

"Where to now?" she asked.

"This way," he said, grimacing. Inwardly, he prayed the emergency stairs were still in one piece all the way to the bottom. At first sight, they seemed to be, but Hao realized he had a bigger problem. "Laura, it's going to take me forever to get down there. If you want to save your son, you're going to have to go on ahead without me."

Fear reflected in her eyes, but she set her jaw and nodded.

She's got guts, this one, he had to admit.

"Listen," he said. "You have to reach the seventh floor, then cross the hangar where the spacecraft is located. You'll find another set of stairs on the other side. It leads to the eighth sub-level. That's where your son is."

She nodded again, wordlessly.

"Be very careful," he cautioned. "We don't know what's down there."

"Be careful, too," she said, before heading away.

"Laura!" Hao hissed, suddenly remembering something. "Check sub-level six. See if the control room is functioning. If security cameras are still active, they might give you an idea as to what's going on down there."

Her eyes widened, but she gestured that she understood, then set off again, with Hao hopping after her at tortoise speed.

* * *

Ben listened to the silence with increasing dread. He expected Bordock's spacecraft to emerge from the hole at any moment. Then the shapeshifter would come for him...

...and that would be the end of me.

He became aware of Beetrix again, anxiously calling his name from nearby. He let the translation skill take over his thoughts and slipped weakly onto the bee's back.

The ground was littered with leaves and broken twigs; the large branch that had landed on the van lay to its side.

He realized that Beetrix wasn't moving, but hovered in one spot. She scanned his mind worriedly, testing his resilience.

Your spirit is frail.

Her statement frightened him because he knew she was right.

Come, she said, lifting upwards into the leaves.

Where are you going?

She didn't answer but used a warm breeze to carry her higher and higher until they reached the summit of the trees.

Beetrix! Where are you going?

* * *

Laura ran down the emergency stairs two steps at a time, swinging around corners with the help of the railing.

Lights flickered on and off. One bulb fizzed just as she rushed by and sparks flew over her head.

She ignored her thumping heart as she wondered what she would find around each corner, then came to a standstill when she spotted a sign that indicated she had reached the sixth floor.

She pushed the door open and glanced down the dark corridor. It was littered with rubble. Not daring to stop for fear she would give in to cowardice, Laura rushed to her right. Not finding anything, she backtracked and headed left.

Double doors, which hung twisted at the hinges, showed promise, and a fallen sign confirmed it was the control room. She hurried inside and found herself in a large room with a broken window to the right and television screens to the left. Wiping away beads of sweat on her forehead, she approached the window slowly, pieces of glass crunching under her feet.

Not far below, the dark form of the humming spacecraft made her skin crawl. She stepped back, willing her mind to focus on what needed to be done.

She turned and glanced at the many screens, half of which showed static. Unstable images scrolled across some other screens. She rushed over to study them, then gasped. A grainy image showed a room with several forms lying next to each other. One of them was Ben.

She touched the screen as if willing herself to pass to the other side, overcome by a mixture of relief at seeing him, but also distressed at the lack of a sign of any life.

She was about to go find her son when a movement caught her eye on another screen. She leaned forward for a better look, then realized the form belonged to Mesmo. The alien lay on the ground, surrounded by rubble. There was a gyrating switch next to the camera, which allowed her to move the camera from left to right. When she did so, a corner of the spacecraft came into view.

Gotcha! she thought to herself, having pinpointed his location, then hurried to find her way down.

She entered the emergency stairs once more but found that the wall had crumbled over the last set of steps. She wasted precious minutes clambering over blocks of concrete and iron poles, coughing her way through the dust that hadn't settled yet.

The final door had burst out of its frame and lay useless on the floor. Slightly disoriented, Laura figured she would find Mesmo to her left, so she avoided the hangar altogether and crept along the wall until she found the spot she had seen on the security screen.

She listened to the muffled silence, her breath coming out too fast. Then she heard a groan.

* * *

Beetrix headed away from the gaping hole and over the treetops, with Ben begging her to turn back.

He fell silent as he became aware of a humming sound from within the branches of a maple tree that towered above the others. It was a comforting, welcoming noise that made him feel safe. He knew before they even reached it that Beetrix was leading him to her hive.

What are you all doing here?

Hadn't he left the hive back at the park?

We followed you and clung on to the roof of the manmade machine that took away your lifeless body. You promised to help us, remember?

We couldn't let you come to harm. We needed to know if you were still alive.

Ben felt a wave of agreement from the swarming insects. Although they buzzed around noisily in a chaotic manner, he sensed an inner harmony that allowed them to speak in one voice. He was reminded that Beetrix had told him about an invisible interconnectedness between hives, and the deathly silence that remained when entire colonies disappeared. He couldn't imagine how horrible it would feel if this hive went silent.

He sensed thoughts of wellbeing and encouragement wash over him as if extended family had decided to visit him in hospital at the same time and were wishing him a swift recovery in unison.

I'm not alone.

A gush of gratefulness almost pulled Ben back into the quicksand's arms, and he had to concentrate for several minutes to settle his emotions.

The humming song lulled him, but a persistent thought kept on pushing him to remain present.

I can't let Bordock win.

The idea escaped him, then slipped into the swirling black hole of quicksand that grated beneath him.

Beetrix, don't let that spaceship leave. Get soldiers... to stop... the shapeshifter...

There were gaps in his thoughts, the pressure exerted by Bordock's trap almost too heavy to bear. At the same time, he sensed that Beetrix was reaching some kind of consensus; one he wanted to be part of. So, with superhuman effort, he willed himself back into the centre of the hive and forced himself to concentrate. The queen bee did not involve him, but the determined buzzing suddenly made him aware of what she was doing.

Beetrix! Don't you dare attack Bordock!

The zooming became muted, and Ben understood that the bee colony had already accepted the challenge. His mind did a double take.

Beetrix! I forbid it!

The queen bee turned her attention to him.

My children were born soldiers. They have poison inside of them and will not survive. They know that they are doomed. That is why they are willing to risk their lives for you, so future colonies might survive. It has been decided.

Ben burst in anger with the last mental strength he could muster, *NO! I won't allow it! Don't...*

Something yanked at him.

I... I won't... You... you c-can't...

Benjamin Archer...?

Beetrix's thoughts faded.

Ben fell. His thoughts scattered at the violent tug that sent him reeling into the black hole. He slipped through the dark quicksand so fast he barely had time to open his mouth in shock.

He choked as his spirit collided heavily with something. He opened his eyes, letting out a halted scream. Someone held his wrists tightly, waving his glowing hands before his face.

"I knew it!" Bordock said with an icy voice, his face hovering inches away from Ben's. "You're trying to use the skill on me."

Ben heard something click.

"Not this time," the shapeshifter snarled, and everything went black.

* * *

Clambering over a fallen column, Laura almost stepped headlong into a deep hole. She gasped and pulled back, then spotted a movement to her right.

"Mesmo!" she cried, climbing over the rubble.

She dropped to her knees by his side. His face was deathly pale, dust covered his cheeks and hands, but he was alive. Laura examined his body for injuries and found his legs trapped in a gap between two slabs of concrete.

Mesmo blinked. "Laura," he gasped. "You shouldn't be here."

"Stay still. I'll get you out." She glanced at his legs worriedly.

Mesmo looked down as well and tried to move. "I can feel my legs," he said. "But they're stuck."

Laura exhaled silently, relieved that he was in one piece. All she had to do was remove one of the slabs and free him. *Easier said than done.* She grabbed at both ends of the slab, pulling with all her might. It barely moved an inch.

"I found Ben," she said, trying to sound calm as she grunted under the effort. "He's one floor down, but I think he's unconscious."

Mesmo tried to help her lift the slab. "Bordock has him," he said. "He has the spirit portal and is stopping Ben's spirit from reuniting with his body."

Laura glanced at him with fearful eyes.

He tried to sound reassuring. "We have to weaken Bordock's willpower over Ben. All Ben needs is a fraction of a second to escape."

Laura avoided eye contact. *Is that all?*

Mesmo must have noticed he wasn't helping because he added, "As soon as I'm out of here I'll get my hands on the spirit portal myself."

She nodded and concentrated on the slab with more determination. She groaned under the effort of pulling at its weight. It moved somewhat, but not enough.

Mesmo sank back, panting, then grabbed her by the arm. His attention had turned to a spot higher up.

She whirled around.

The outline of a man dwarfed them from above the fallen column. His hands glowed.

Laura yelled in shock and scampered away.

Bordock hopped down lightly from the column and landed on the very slab they had been trying to move seconds ago. His cold eyes were set on Mesmo.

CHAPTER 20 *Broken Trust*

"Fancy a test of skills?" Bordock sneered, his hands glowing brighter. His mouth curled into a smile. "Ah, but you seem a little *out of your element...*"

"No!" Laura begged, guessing his intentions.

Bordock turned hard eyes on her. "Still confused, are we? But, that's right, Laura Archer. I made you a deal. I promised you this Toreq scum would tell you the truth before I finish him off."

Laura suppressed a whimper.

The shapeshifter stared at Mesmo again. "How about it? She deserves to know, don't you think?"

"Bordock..." Mesmo protested.

"Tell her!" Bordock shouted, his face twisting in anger. "I want to hear you say it! Tell her who you are! Tell her why you're here!"

A thick, threatening silence fell over the two men as they glared at each other.

Laura stared at them, terrified. "Mesmo?" she said in a tiny voice. "Tell me what?"

Mesmo's facial features sagged. He wouldn't meet her eyes. Finally, he said, "Do you remember, when I told you about the Great War of the Kins?"

Laura nodded stiffly.

"Many eons ago, the Toreq and the A'hmun fought the greatest war in their known history and almost annihilated each other in the process. But the Toreq came out victorious. After much debate, my people decided to banish the surviving enemy." He dropped his chin to his chest. "The Toreq banished the A'hmun to a lost pebble in the confines of space, with limited resources and isolated from any cluster of civilized planets..." His voice drifted off.

Laura crossed her arms over her stomach. She glanced at Bordock, who examined her reaction with glee. She found it harder and harder to breathe.

"Do you get it now?" Bordock said in a low voice. "That lost pebble is Earth. And humans *are* the A'hmun."

Laura shook her head in full denial.

Bordock smirked. "That's right. The human race is all that is left of the Toreq's most feared enemies. You descend from the A'hmun. You were placed on this meaningless planet a million years ago as punishment, your memories wiped clean, and this so-called *friend* of yours is here to determine whether you are still worthy of this rock, or whether you should be exterminated once and for all."

Laura took a step back, almost tripping over her own feet. Her eyes darted from one to the other, hoping for some sort of rebuttal. When none came, she breathed in disbelief, "Mesmo?"

Mesmo looked away. "It's true. The Toreq have kept an eye on Earth for millennia. The Wise Ones keep track of human progress, and every two hundred years, an Observer is sent from the Mother Planet to collect information on them.

"We have never forgotten that, once, the Toreq and the A'hmun were like brothers, and we have maintained the faint hope that maybe, one day, the A'hmun and their descendants would develop into a wiser, more respectful civilization—one that would allow us to put our differences aside and make peace."

Bordock snorted. "That's never going to

happen, of course. Humans are on the brink of space travel. They are already reaching out to other planets in their solar system. Within the next two hundred years, they will have settled on surrounding moons and planets. By the time the next wormhole opens, humans will have the means to cross it."

He grimaced. "The Toreq will never allow it. They can't allow a species that is responsible for the loss of seventy percent of plant and animal life on this planet to spread to other galaxies. Pure greed lives in their blood. It is this greed that sparked the Great War of the Kins. The A'hmun have not changed."

Laura's mouth fell open. She glared at Mesmo. "Is that why you needed Ben's skill? To find out what the animals have to say about us? And he told you they are on the brink of extinction because of us?"

Mesmo nodded.

Bordock gave a hollow laugh. "Your son has doomed the human race. That is..." he hissed, his eyes boring into Mesmo's, "...unless we stop this scum from getting away."

Tears spilled down Laura's cheeks. She couldn't believe the treachery. "You said..." she sobbed. "You said you weren't interested in Earth."

Mesmo set his jaw. "Not Earth, no. But humans, yes."

"I told you, Laura Archer," Bordock quipped. "I told you not to trust him. But you wouldn't listen."

Laura's cheeks burned. "Don't you dare judge me! You are no better than he is when it comes to deceit. Release Ben at once and show me which side you're on!"

A smile crept on to Bordock's face as if she had just cracked a joke.

"She's right," Mesmo followed. "Which side are you on, Bordock? Are you A'hmun? Or are you Toreq?"

"I am both," he said, sniffing. "My physical appearance has allowed me to blend into the Toreq world, but my A'hmun side has always been a burden. I have lived my life hiding my bloodline from the Toreq. So, when the opportunity presented itself, I volunteered to come to this trivial planet to terminate the Observer's mission, away from Toreq eyes. Because, you see, humans must be saved if they are ever to defeat the Toreq and occupy their rightful place on the Mother Planet."

"Really?" Mesmo spoke sharply. "And who are you *volunteering* for? Who sent you? What did they promise you?" He paused, then gasped. "They promised you legal Toreq status, didn't they?"

Bordock's smile wavered.

Mesmo pressed on. "No Toreq in their right mind would have allowed you to do the vile things you did. And yet you show no fear in returning to the Mother Planet. Someone is protecting you. Whoever sent you must be powerful indeed."

Bordock's face hardened. "This conversation is boring me." His hands began to glow again. "This is as far as you go, Observer."

"Hey! Wonder boy!"

Bordock whirled.

Hao stood behind him. The Inspector swung one of his crutches at Bordock and hit him square in the stomach.

The alien keeled over, losing control of his power. Blue lightning burst out of his hands with a deafening bang, sending Laura and Hao sprawling.

Laura hit the floor with a humph. Her mind swam toward unconsciousness from the impact, but she forced herself to sit up, fighting the ringing in her ears. Through watery eyes, she registered that Hao was also coming to, though not fast enough.

The shapeshifter had picked himself up. His

spikey, white hair disappeared; his neck twisted. By the time he had straightened, Bordock had turned back into the bald Connelly once more.

Hao cringed at the sight.

Connelly smirked. "You got me there, *partner*," he panted, clinging to his stomach. "You should have stayed buried under that avalanche. But no matter, I'd rather finish you off myself." He lunged at Hao, reaching for his neck.

Hao gagged and struggled.

Dazedly, Laura watched Hao and Connelly scuffling dangerously close to the hole that she had narrowly avoided falling into earlier. She could tell Hao was wearing out.

Something small buzzed before her face and landed on her arm.

Mesmo, who continued to pull at his legs to try and free them from under the slab, saw it, too. It was a bee. "It's Ben!" he exclaimed.

Laura's heart leapt. *He's alive!*

Then, following the first bee, an angry hum came closer and closer. Laura lifted her head just in time to see a mass of bees come bearing down on them. She ducked as thousands of them darted by her, heading straight for Connelly. The black tornado drowned the two battling men, who waved their arms in a useless attempt to swipe the insects away.

The shapeshifter screamed.

Then, in a heartstopping moment, one of the men teetered and slipped off the ledge while the other stumbled to the ground, succumbing to the angry mob of tiny attackers.

A cry stuck in her throat. Laura crawled to the edge and glanced over the side with dread.

Hao hung from the ledge with one hand, groaning under the effort not to let go.

"I've got you!" she yelled, reaching for his wrist. But doubt washed over her as she grabbed his arm and realized she wasn't strong enough to pull him up. She caught sight of sharp concrete blocks in the dark pit below Hao.

She lay down on her stomach and held on with all her might as Hao desperately tried to reach for the ledge with his other hand.

Suddenly, a strong arm lowered beside Laura, took over her grasp of the Inspector, and with one mighty pull, extracted Hao from his precarious plight. The Inspector clambered out of the hole, wincing, and rolled on to his back to see who had saved him.

Both he and Laura stared up at Mesmo, who stood over them. The alien man had managed to push the concrete slab that had pinned his legs to the side.

Bordock lay unmoving in a heap a few feet away. Hao dragged himself up to the shapeshifter and felt for a pulse, then shook his head. "He's gone," he said. "Bees got him good." He checked his hands and face. "I don't have a single bee sting," he noted.

Laura winced at the sight of the shapeshifter's swollen face. A dozen insects rose before her face and buzzed away. She lifted her hand, feeling bumps underneath it, only to realize they belonged to crushed bees. She glanced around as she stood in a hurry and found she was lying on a thin carpet of crumpled insects.

They died protecting us, she realized in horror. *Ben must have sent them!*

She raised her palm with the dead bees cradled inside, her eyes falling on the alien who had once been her friend. Her heart constricted. Fighting anger and grief, she caught her breath and dashed past him.

"Laura, wait!" Mesmo called, his feet thudding after her.

She was no match for his long legs. He grabbed her by the arm.

"Don't touch me!" she yelled, struggling. "I need to find Ben!"

"Ben is fine!" Mesmo said, holding her tightly. "Look." He pointed at Bordock's arm. The silver watch lay with its glass shattered, the tiny spirit portal broken in three pieces, their glimmer gone.

"Bordock's power over Ben's spirit is gone," Mesmo said. "Ben will be waking as we speak."

Just then a massive slab of concrete detached itself from the roof and crashed to the ground not far from them, sending rocks and dust flying. Mesmo rushed to cover her head with his arms, but she pushed him away.

"Leave me alone!" she shouted, her nostrils flaring. "You deceived me! And Ben, oh God, Ben! How could you?"

Mesmo responded, "Did I, really?"

"You lied to us! You used us!" she sobbed. From way up on the surface, she heard soldiers shouting orders, indicating that they were beginning their descent into the Dugout.

"Get away from me!" she yelled angrily. "Go, then!" She was no longer trying to save him. She wanted him out of her sight forever.

He watched her sob, then lowered his eyes and took a step back. He nodded slowly. Walking in a circle around her, he heaved Bordock over his shoulder, glanced at her once more, then turned his back, and left.

She watched him walk away, wiping at her tear-filled cheeks, then bent shakily to help Hao to his feet. They followed the alien from a distance.

Mesmo reached the spaceship, activated its door and dumped Bordock inside.

Laura could hear pounding feet resounding from somewhere high up, and a helicopter's strong light beam swiped past them, its rotor blades causing more red mist to swirl to the surface. Mesmo stood illuminated by the inside of the spacecraft, glancing back at them.

Her heart leapt in her throat. She released Hao beside a column so he could lean on it and stepped forward, but he held her back.

"Don't!" he cautioned.

Oblivious to his warning, she crossed the hangar, clambering over debris, until she was facing Mesmo. Without taking defiant eyes off him, she pulled the two treble clef symbols from her pocket and shoved them into his hand.

Her chin trembling, she said, "Take these, and do with them what you will. If we truly are the terrible species you claim we are, then all my efforts will have been in vain. But at least, I'll know I have nothing to be ashamed of. At least I tried."

Mesmo jerked his head as if she had said

something significant. He set his jaw and took her hand. "Come with me," he said firmly. "You and Ben. You have nothing to fear of the Toreq. I will speak a good word for you. You would be welcome on the Mother Planet."

Laura recoiled. "You would save Ben and me, but destroy the rest of the human race—as if we were different from anyone else? How could you think I would ever accept such a thing?" She could tell her words hurt him. *Good!*

"Who said anything about destroying anything, Laura Archer? Don't let the shapeshifter's words play with your mind." He lifted the side of his shirt and waved at the bare skin with a glowing hand.

Laura gaped as some of his skin became transparent, revealing a hidden row of treble clefs. He pushed the remaining two into place next to the five other ones, and they melted into his skin. "I don't know what these contain. I have not analyzed their data yet. Nothing is set in stone."

He glanced at her. "But one thing is certain: if the Toreq do not hear from me before the wormhole closes, then it is certain that they will send a military fleet to investigate." He paused. "The only way to stop them is for me to return to the Mother Planet."

Laura shut her eyes and shook her head. "And what will you tell them? That an A'hmun shapeshifter killed your wife and daughter, that a human held you captive, that my son told you the animals are sick and dying... How could the Toreq ever forgive us? How could you ever forgive us? We may have sealed our fate, but our fate is our own, and you have no right to meddle with it."

"Yes," he said. "What you say is true. Human greed is destroying the world we entrusted to them. But then, there's you, and there's Ben, your father, Susan, Kimimela... I have met the best and the worst of your species. The Toreq will place all this in the balance."

Laura hung her head, unable to hear more. In a broken voice, she whispered, "You broke my heart."

She heard him catch his breath. His hands went limp by his side, and his voice came out thick and low. "Do you see, now, why I told you I cannot love you?"

Her eyes widened as she met his.

He stared at her, meaningfully. "Now that you know the truth, knowing what you know, could you still love me, Laura Archer?"

Her lips trembled.

Strong flashlights swung past them from

above. "Freeze!" voices shouted a couple of floors up.

"Goodbye, Laura," Mesmo said. "Tell Benjamin I'm sorry." He stepped back, his eyes on her the whole time. He entered the spacecraft, faced her and raised his hand.

For a split second, she thought he hesitated, but then he flicked his hand and the door shut between them.

Laura pressed a fist to her mouth as she edged away. "Goodbye," she whispered, tears streaming down her face.

* * *

The door closed behind Mesmo. Sounds became muffled through the ship's thick walls. He activated the front window and found a rain of whizzing bullets pelting the vessel. He caught a last glimpse of Laura as she sought cover.

Turning his attention to the inside of the vessel, Mesmo picked up the shapeshifter and dragged him into a cubicle at the back of the ship, then activated an electrical barrier to lock him in.

He took his place at the front of the ship, his body and hands accommodating automatically to surroundings that were natural to him.

Pressing a couple of commands, he activated the departure mechanism and felt a satisfactory jolt as the spacecraft came to life. Without a sound, the vessel lifted from the ground, making the remaining red mist swirl around it. It fit perfectly through the hole, sending soldiers scrambling to upper levels. The dark ship emerged at the surface and faced a squadron of army trucks, tankers and helicopters.

Unfazed, Mesmo switched to hyperspeed and arrived in a layer of clouds in a matter of milliseconds. Human combat aircraft pursued him for some time but were no match for his speed.

He entered the outer atmosphere and floated there for some time, taking in the curve of the planet, the outline of the continents and the blue of the oceans.

Then, with a heart that suffered as much as when his wife and daughter had died, he checked his trajectory and sped off into the far reaches of space.

* * *

Laura watched from a safe distance as the spacecraft ascended into the night, her throat tight.

Hao hopped over to her. They watched the gaping hole with the red mist swirling upward. "You let him go," he said in awe.

Laura bit her trembling lip. "If not Mesmo, then it will be another Observer. And whether now or in the future, eventually, humans will have to face the Toreq."

Hao squeezed her shoulder. "We will be ready," he vowed.

Laura gave him a small nod, feeling empty inside. "I need to find Ben," she said.

Hao puffed his cheeks. "Let's go, then." He turned and led her to the stairs leading to the last floor, making it down after some painstaking minutes. Hao clearly suffered from multiple injuries, but Laura guessed he wanted to see her through to the end.

"In here," he said, pointing to the sealed room that contained the incubators.

She entered and squinted at the gloom, while emergency lights flickered on and off. The first incubators were empty. "Ben?" she called, rushing to the back, where she had seen him lying on a stretcher on one of the security screens.

The stretcher was there, but not Ben.

She panicked. Mesmo had said he would be

awake by now. She glanced around frantically. "Ben? Where are you?"

There wasn't a sound.

A wave of nausea washed over her. "No!" she gasped, cold dread gripping her. "NO!"

She swivelled on her heels, rushed past Hao, and bolted up the stairs two steps at a time. She froze at the center of the gaping hole, lifted her head to the sky and screamed, *"BEN!"*

CHAPTER 21 *Paradox*

The spacecraft skimmed by Earth's Moon, but Mesmo did not see it. He darkened the front window and concentrated on several screens that he had pulled up before him. Different coloured lights flickered, symbols scrolled down the sides, and intricate patterns turned on of their own accord.

He activated the hidden pocket that stuck to his skin. The neat row of seven keys appeared. He stared at them. All the keys were there, yes, but at what cost?

Too many deaths...

He pulled out the first one, examined it, then inserted it into a slot on the dashboard. A waterfall of information gushed before him. Minutes turned into hours, and hours into days, as he analyzed the data on each key, the spacecraft speeding through the darkness towards its inevitable destination.

The equivalent of ten Earth days passed during which time Mesmo scanned six of the keys.

The information contained in them was not good. Once his people were in possession of the data, he knew the Toreq would vote to put an end to the human race before they had time to spread to other galaxies like a cancer. The risk of this species multiplying and then depleting other planets' resources before having learned to respect boundaries was real. The Toreq had seen it before, during the time leading up to the Great War of the Kins, and would not allow it to happen again. Clearly, banishing the A'hmun to Earth a million years ago to give them a last chance to better themselves had not been successful.

The Toreq would vote against the survival of the A'hmun's descendants, they would sacrifice a handful of warships by sending them through the wormhole before it closed, and annihilation would begin.

Mesmo sat back and sighed, only too aware that, not long ago, he would have supported this decision unequivocally.

But that was before he had met Ben and Laura...

He travelled back in his mind to the steps of the Kalasasaya temple in Bolivia. The Wise One called Amaru had delivered a scathing report on humans and yet, when Mesmo had indicated that the Toreq would save him should they attack, Amaru had refused. He preferred to remain on Earth and share the fate of humans.

Mesmo had not understood it then, but he did now.

Amaru had already seen the doubt that clouded Mesmo's judgement from having had too much contact with the A'hmun descendants.

"The Observer is no longer neutral."

With Amaru's words hanging like a dirty smudge in his mind, Mesmo collected the last key and stared at it for a moment, before slipping it into the last slot.

He dozed off while sifting through the data, waking with a start to a crackling sound. A smooth, metallic voice filled the spacecraft. The words were unintelligible to human ears, yet Mesmo's brow relaxed.

"Receiving signal," the placid voice stated. "Identify."

Mesmo let out a shaky breath. "This is Earth

Mission. Observer reporting."

There was a long silence, and Mesmo knew he had just unleashed great excitement on the other side.

"Mesmo? Is that you?"

Because his contact had called him by name, Mesmo already knew who it was. "Yes, Torka."

Another silence.

"We feared the worst," Torka's calm voice resonated in the ship. "What happened? I don't recognize your vessel's signature."

Mesmo's face became sombre. "The Earth Mission was attacked by an A'hmun rebel. I lost my two vessels... and my crew." He paused. "Rebel is dead. This is his vessel. I am the sole survivor." He stopped talking, reflecting on the failure of his mission. He had the seven keys, yes, but there had been too many deaths.

This time it took several minutes for Torka to get back to him. Mesmo waited expectantly for the metallic voice that came from his Mother Planet.

"Opening channel to receive data," Torka said. "The Arch Council is ready to debate the fate of the banished A'hmun. Our forces are gathered at the wormhole..."

"I'm not sure *A'hmun* is still the appropriate

name for the peoples' of Earth," Mesmo reflected half to himself.

"The Arch Council awaits the keys," the voice interrupted.

Mesmo stared at the seven slots without moving.

"Wormhole closing in four-one units," Torka continued. "Trajectory stable. Confirm transfer of data..." There was a pause, then Torka added, "...and identify the vessel's second occupant."

Mesmo's head shot up at Torka's last words. "Repeat?" he exclaimed.

The voice came through evenly, yet it turned Mesmo's blood cold. "We are capturing a second heartbeat in your vessel. Identify."

Mesmo whirled. He stared at Bordock, but the shapeshifter had not moved. Yet, Torka maintained there was someone else in the vessel with him. Searching feverishly, his gaze fell on the six, large circles outlined on the back wall of the ship—three above and three below. He jumped to his feet and scanned them with his eyes. Tiny lights scintillated next to each tube. A heartbeat registered in one of them.

The voice insisted behind him, "Identify."

Mesmo touched the flickering light with his

fingertip, and a sleep-inducing tube slid out effortlessly before him.

Mesmo gaped at the boy within.

* * *

Ben opened his eyes. The contour of a man's strong features hovered above his own.

"Mesmo!" he gasped. He straightened into a sitting position and threw himself into the alien's arms.

Mesmo almost fell over, but caught himself just in time, then hugged him back. "Benjamin!" he exclaimed. "What are you doing here?"

Ben hiccupped into Mesmo's shoulder. "It was Bordock. He brought our bodies to the spaceship, then broke the connection with the spirit portal. I barely registered slipping back into my body before I lost consciousness. I thought you were... I..." The words wouldn't come as emotion overwhelmed him.

Mesmo pulled him to a standing position, staring at him with eyebrows drawn together. Ben wondered why his face had turned ashen, but the alien pulled him close and hugged him tightly.

Ben sniffled into the alien's sweater. "I'm so glad to see you!" he said. "I thought I was done for."

"Oh, Benjamin, you have no idea..." Mesmo said, unable to finish the sentence.

They held on a while longer in silence, but then Mesmo let him go and said, "Wait a minute. You said Bordock brought our bodies. Do you mean...?" He broke off and rushed to the other sleep-inducing tubes. He activated them, one after the other, until the six tubes had slid out before them. Two were empty, but three contained lifeless forms.

Ben squinted as both he and Mesmo were drawn to the same tube. It held a young girl with long, white hair. Mesmo grasped the side of the tube, stooping over his daughter.

"Kaia!" he breathed in a broken voice.

Ben stood by him, his throat tight, and observed the delicate features and greyish skin of the one who had given him his skill.

It could have been me.

His legs feeling wobbly, Ben sank to a crouching position. He leaned with his back against the wall of the ship and bent his head in silence while Mesmo spread his arms over Kaia's tube and rested his forehead against the glass.

They remained like that for a long time, until a robotic voice crackled through the craft.

"What's that?" Ben jumped in alarm.

Mesmo slowly released the tube. "Home," he said.

"Wha...?" He stood in a hurry, excitement washing over him. "You can actually communicate with someone on your home planet, on the other side of the wormhole?"

Mesmo nodded grimly and sent the tubes containing their precious cargo back into the wall.

The voice repeated the same thing.

"What's he saying?" Ben whispered in awe.

Mesmo looked at him. "They want to know who's with me."

Ben gulped, suddenly feeling observed. "Oh," was all he could come up with, then spotted a form hunched in a corner. He gasped in fear. "Mesmo! Is that...?"

Mesmo turned and approached the lifeless shapeshifter. He deactivated the electrical barrier, bent to his knees and nudged at the alien with the tips of his fingers. "...Bordock, yes," he confirmed.

"What happened to him?" Ben breathed.

Mesmo turned to him and frowned, but instead of answering, he said, "Ben, your hands!"

Ben lifted them and found that they glowed.

A tired voice entered his mind.

Hello, Benjamin Archer. I am happy to see

that you are awake.

"Whoa!" Ben exclaimed as Beetrix lifted from Bordock's form and landed on the palm of his hand.

Beetrix! Am I glad to see you! I was afraid you were going to do something stupid.

The queen bee fluttered her tiny wings without replying.

Beetrix?

She remained silent, and Ben sensed her crushing exhaustion.

"Mesmo, what happened to Bordock?" he asked with fear growing in the pit of his stomach.

Mesmo frowned. "What do you mean? Don't you know?"

"How could I? I was in there." He gestured to the tubes.

Mesmo's eyes narrowed. "You mean, you don't know what happened *at all?*"

Ben shook his head, tears welling in his eyes. "No, but I can already guess. Beetrix sent her hive on Bordock, didn't she?"

"Yes, but why are you sad? Aren't you the one who ordered the attack?"

Ben's nostrils flared. "Of course not!" He turned accusing eyes to the queen bee. "Beetrix, I told you not to do that! Why didn't you listen?"

His voice shook as he turned to Mesmo again. "Don't you see? When a bee stings, it dies. It can only sting once. Beetrix sacrificed her hive to save us from Bordock."

"I'm aware of that. But isn't that what you wanted?"

Ben shut his eyes. "Argh! No, no! I told Beetrix not to do that. But she went ahead anyway..."

"Benjamin." Ben opened his eyes and found Mesmo with his head tilted. "If the hive hadn't attacked Bordock, we would probably be dead by now. Are you saying they came of their own, free will?"

Ben was crushed. He stared at Beetrix and nodded.

Mesmo continued, "With the skill you possess, you could have told the bees to save you, even if it meant sacrificing them. You could have imposed your will on them." His voice softened. "But you didn't."

Ben sat and rested his head in his hands. "Of course not. I would never ask that of anyone—or anything—to risk their life for me."

"Even if it meant losing yours..." Mesmo's voice trailed off.

Ben exhaled into his hands.

Benjamin Archer. Those I lost were soldiers who were raised to protect me. They knew that my future hive will only survive if you do, too. I ask you to speak to your kind on my behalf. You must tell them that the connection between bee colonies is broken. We are lost and confused. Our children are sick. My hive is lost, but, with your help, other hives will thrive.

Ben slowly slid his head out of his hands and nodded.

Yes, Beetrix, I promised I would help. And I will.

The insect buzzed.

Then let us get out of this box. I need sunlight.

"What is she saying?" Mesmo asked, observing Ben.

Ben forced a smile. "She says she wants out. Can we get some fresh air?"

The metallic voice burst into the spacecraft, and floating screens went wild with symbols.

"Now what?" Ben exclaimed as he watched the swirling patterns reflecting on the black walls of the ship.

Mesmo remained still as stone, taking no notice of what the spacecraft was telling him. Although the otherworldly voice spoke evenly, its continued repetitions made it clear that something was up.

"Mesmo?" Ben felt pressure mounting. "What's he saying?"

Finally, Mesmo looked him straight in the eyes. "He is saying that we have arrived."

Ben raised an eyebrow. "Arrived... where?"

The alien flicked his hand, and the hovering screens vanished, leaving them in total darkness, but then Ben realized the window had cleared, revealing tiny pinpricks of light on the other side. He bent forward. "Wow! Are those stars?" He glanced at Mesmo, his heart pounding, "Are we *flying*?"

The alien stared at him intensely, and Ben's mouth went dry. "Wait a minute..." he said, staring at the darkness again.

The spacecraft tipped, and a massive planet rose before him, filling the entire window. Brown lines swirled around its yellowish surface while the vessel hurtled under billions of icy rocks that made up row after row of rings that circled it.

Ben's eyes almost rolled out of their sockets. "Is... is th-that...?"

"Saturn."

Ben lost his voice altogether. He pressed his hands and nose against the window, his eyes not big enough to take in the immensity of the view that sprawled before him.

The spacecraft glided to the left, revealing the crackled surface of another globe, this one a beautiful bluish-grey, with wrinkles that resembled rivers.

"And that is Enceladus," Mesmo said, though Ben's ears refused to transfer the unbelievable information to his brain.

The spacecraft slid towards Saturn's moon, and Ben began making out translucent plumes of water vapor emanating from the celestial body. As the ship approached the surface and entered one of the plumes, a gush of tiny ice particles hit the window like glitter, making Ben jump.

The spacecraft emerged from the geyser of ice and headed for another particularly long one that reached out in Saturn's direction, then swirled mid-way and disappeared into nothingness like water going down a drain.

The metallic voice spoke incessantly, with Mesmo answering in a guttural language.

"What did you say?" he asked in awe.

Mesmo did not answer right away. "I told them," he said finally, "that my cold analysis of the data leads me to conclude that the A'hmun deserve to be crushed once and for all, yet my heart aches to embrace each and every one of them individually..."

Ben lifted an eyebrow, not understanding.

Mesmo seemed to have forgotten that he was standing there, and said half to himself, "How does one mend such a paradox?"

Ben opened his mouth to speak, but the alien said, "Approaching wormhole in zero-seven units. Wormhole closure in three-one units."

"Wormhole?" Ben managed, his voice tiny. He could barely stand on his legs. He blinked at the approaching, swirling geyser that was sucked into the pinpoint of a wormhole and forced the words out of his mouth, his heart sinking all the way to his feet as the realization hit him. "You don't have time to take me back to Earth, do you?"

He turned slowly to face Mesmo, who stared at him with intense eyes. The alien's subdued voice sounded far away. "I didn't know you were on the vessel, Benjamin. If I had known..."

Ben closed his eyes as dizziness grasped him. He opened them again and knew instantly that he and Mesmo were sharing the same, overwhelming thought.

One of us is never going home.

CHAPTER 22 *Return*

The doorbell chimed through the dark house. Laura, who lay fully clothed on the sofa where her father had placed an unconscious Mesmo so many months back, pulled herself upright with difficulty. Her hair was in a mess, and dark pockets cradled her green eyes.

She forced herself to the door, pulled the knob and squinted at the sunlight. She hadn't opened the curtains in three weeks.

Inspector Hao stood before her, his car parked in the driveway of her father's house. A black-and-white English Shepherd tugged at its leash, its tongue lolling in excitement. "Sit still, Buddy," Hao said.

The dog sat obediently, grinning at his

master.

Hao's eyebrows knitted together as he glanced at Laura.

"Any news?" she blurted, unable to contain herself.

Hao shook his head.

Even though the sun was shining, she pulled her cardigan closer about her and sunk her chin into it so he couldn't see it quiver. She sniffed and moved aside. "Come on in." Her voice sounded tired.

Hao cleared his throat. "Actually, do you mind joining me outside? Buddy has been cooped up in the car far too long. I think he'd like to go for a run."

Laura nodded and stepped outside reluctantly, closing the door behind her.

They walked side-by-side—Hao limping somewhat—until they reached the fields where young corn crops reached shoulder height. The late morning was crisp and clean, and Laura could see across the valley to the mountains on the other side. She swallowed a lump in her throat and almost headed back inside, but Buddy sprang before her, barking excitedly and asking to be patted. Laura obliged. Then, the English Shepherd took off down the fields happily.

"I was at a funeral in Chilliwack this morning," Hao spoke gently. "We combed the Dugout from top to bottom. And we found something... or more accurately... someone," he explained.

Her eyes widened.

Hao sighed. "We found the remains of Agent Theodore Edmond Connelly. The real Connelly. We think Bordock must have kept him in the spaceship all along, then dumped him in the Dugout in the end."

Buddy came back for a pat, then broke away again.

"He was laid to rest this morning with great honours. His wife, Tamara Connelly, will receive government compensation. Hopefully, she will find some peace knowing her husband didn't abandon her, but died a hero."

Laura continued to cover her mouth with her cardigan. She knew he was watching her.

"I'm sorry," he continued. "I wish you could have that kind of closure."

She nodded in thanks, unable to speak, but now tears popped into her eyes.

They watched Buddy for some time, then Hao said, "I have been named Head of the National Aerial Division of the CSIS."

"I heard," Laura managed, sniffing. "They said on the news that the former High Inspector was arrested on money laundering charges. Something to do with Victor Hayward."

Hao nodded.

"Congratulations," Laura said, trying to sound sincere, but her voice sounded hollow instead.

"Thank you. The point is, I came to tell you that my colleagues are convinced only one alien survived *The Cosmic Fall*, and that he took his deceased companions and escaped Earth in the remaining spacecraft. They don't know about Connelly, or what happened to him. They have no clue there was an alien shapeshifter involved."

He paused. "All this to say that I cleared you and your son's name. You won't be bothered by anyone, Laura. Any contact with the CSIS in the future must pass through me."

He glanced at her meaningfully. "There is much to do if we are to prepare for the return of the Toreq. Convincing governments to prepare for a possible alien strike in a distant future is going to be an impossible undertaking—what with governments squabbling and so few people knowing the truth. But I have to try, and I may need your help when you feel up to it."

Laura glanced at the ground.

I don't feel up to it.

"Take your time," Hao said gently. "It's just something for you to consider."

She nodded.

"I... um...," Hao continued. "I also have another request."

Laura glanced at him questioningly.

He gestured toward the dog. "This new position is going to keep me busy. I'll be travelling a lot. I won't really have time to take care of Buddy. So, I was wondering... you know... would you be willing...?"

The English Shepherd sat beside Laura, gazing up at her lovingly.

She forced a sad smile. "Yes, Inspector, of course. I'll take care of Buddy."

Hao's stance relaxed as if a weight had been removed from his shoulders. "Thank you," he said. "And it's James. None of that Inspector business between us, after what we've been through."

He shifted uncomfortably. "I wanted to apologize, for your son's dog. I would have liked to tell Ben myself, but..."

Laura looked at him in surprise, then said, "It's okay, James. You don't have to apologize. It was Bordock's doing. You were just trying to protect yourself."

Hao nodded grimly. "I'd better get going, then," he said. "I fly back to Toronto tonight." He glanced at her. "Will you be all right?"

No, I won't.

She nodded silently.

They headed back to Hao's car and said their goodbyes.

* * *

Hao glanced in his rearview mirror as he sped off, Laura becoming smaller and smaller. He set his jaw.

How does one get over the loss of a son? he thought sadly.

He didn't think anyone could, including Laura.

Before driving to Ryan Archer's house, he had checked in with NASA for the hundredth time. He had asked the US space program to point their satellites at Saturn and its moons, following Laura's instructions, but the search hadn't turned up anything unusual. A search of the Solar System hadn't revealed any sign of alien life.

He feared the worst for the boy, who, he

realized, had become victim to a war no-one knew anything about.

Reaching a curb, he slowed down to read a large sign that said FOR SALE. The house behind it was Victor Hayward's. The bankruptcy of the billionaire's airliner was forcing him to sell all his properties.

Hao pressed on the gas pedal, but his motor sputtered. He pushed it again, and the car lurched a few feet, before dying. Turning the key in the ignition several times only strained the motor.

Drat!

Hao hit the wheel in exasperation. Shielding his eyes from the bright sun, he skimmed the area, hoping to find someone who could help, but the hillside was empty of life.

He stepped out of the car, lifted the hood, and checked the motor. At first glance, there was nothing wrong with it. Squinting back the way he had come, he wondered how long it would take him to walk back to the Archer house.

Hao sighed and returned to the driver's seat, then grabbed his mobile phone. The line was dead.

What the heck? He thought as he tugged angrily at his sweaty collar, the sun illuminating his dashboard brightly.

He froze. *Wait a minute, that's not the sun!*

He tensed in his seat, then leaned forward to squint through the front windshield. The fake sun dropped from the sky and glided smoothly towards him in a dazzling display of light.

His jaw dropped as the radiant object dimmed and turned into a black craft that floated soundlessly over his car.

* * *

Laura sat on the steps leading to the kitchen. She watched as Buddy sniffed at the ground in the back yard, then uprooted some yellow dandelions with his paws.

The dog straightened suddenly, his dirty snout sniffing the air, where he remained poised like a statue with one paw lifted.

"What is it, Buddy? Did you smell a rabbit?" Laura said, returning her focus on a dandelion she twirled between her fingers.

She heard the dog bark suddenly from far away.

Laura blinked and stood slowly. "Buddy?" she called, realizing he had dashed off without her noticing.

There was no sign of him.

She left the stairs and glanced at the driveway to check if James had come back, but it was empty of cars.

"Buddy!" she shouted at the fields, stretching her neck.

The dog appeared at the end of the path that cut through the cornfields, running wildly towards her. She cocked her head and then shook it, wondering whether she had made a mistake in accepting a dog that she would have to chase all day.

She was about to turn back when a form appeared behind the dog. The person was walking up toward the house, and it was a boy.

Laura clutched her stomach.

It can't be...

She watched, expecting the illusion to disappear in the time of a blink.

But the boy continued to walk down the path. He saw her and waved. "Mom!" he shouted.

Laura lifted her hand to her mouth, afraid to acknowledge the feeling of extreme happiness surging through her body. She took a step forward, then another, and before she knew it, she had broken into a run, crying "Ben!"

They met in the middle of the path and landed in each other's arms so hard that they fell over, laughing. They hugged tightly, giggling and crying at the same time. Buddy sprang around them, barking. Laura wiped a tear from Ben's cheek, leaving a trail of dust.

He grinned at her. "You'll never guess where I was!"

A shadow fell over them and Laura raised her hand to shield her eyes. Mesmo glanced down at them in amusement.

She took Ben by the hand and pulled him to a standing position, then faced the alien. "You came back!" she said, breathless.

Mesmo smiled. "I had to."

She tilted her head, not understanding.

"You see, you didn't answer my question," he said.

"What question?"

He looked at her with his honey-brown eyes. "Now that you know the truth, knowing what you know, could you still love me, Laura Archer?"

She opened her mouth, but no words came out. *Did he really say that?*

He stood before her, waiting.

The release of a long suppressed hope made her heart bulge. Feeling giddy, she broke into a smile and nodded. "Yes. Yes, I can!" she whispered.

They stared at one another, bewildered at seeing each other in flesh and blood again. Then he pulled her into his arms and she welcomed his embrace.

Before long, Ben latched on to them as well, and the three of them hung onto each other like a single pillar rooted to the earth.

* * *

The giant maple tree spread its branches. Its leaves danced in an afternoon breeze, while the cornfields reflected a setting sun.

Mesmo crouched by his daughter's grave and made delicate flowers of ice flow out of a clay jug. When he was done, he sat on a thick, protruding root, leaned his elbows on his knees and placed his head in his hands.

Ben and Laura bowed their head in silent respect.

Crickets chirped and the first star appeared.

Laura placed her arm around Ben's shoulders, and he intertwined his fingers with hers.

"Mesmo sent Bordock's body, as well as that of his companions through the wormhole," Ben whispered. "But he wanted Kaia to return to Earth with him."

Laura remained silent beside him, then said, "He can never go back, can he?"

Ben shook his head. "I don't think so," he whispered. "It was him or me." He bit his lip. "He chose me."

Laura shut her eyes as she squeezed his shoulders.

They stood together for a long moment, until Laura tugged at his arm, indicating they should head home.

Ben knew she wanted to give Mesmo some space, but he wasn't quite ready to go. "I'll come in a minute," he whispered.

She nodded in understanding and headed back to the house with Buddy in the lead.

Ben stared at Kaia's grave for several minutes, thinking about the past events and about the girl he would have liked to know better. How much could she have taught him about the skill? Now, that knowledge was lost.

His hands glowed, and Beetrix landed in his palm. She fluttered her wings.

I will begin a new hive here. It is a good place. You can count on me for help, Benjamin Archer. You will need it.

She buzzed off and disappeared into the

branches of the tree.

Ben sighed and went to sit beside Mesmo without saying a word.

The alien lifted his head from his hands.

"Thank you for bringing me home," Ben said softly, struggling under the weight of knowing what that meant for the alien.

Mesmo remained silent for a minute, then replied, "There is nothing left for me, back there. This is where I belong now."

Ben pursed his lips. "But what did you tell the Toreq? What was on the seven keys?"

"More bad, than good," he said. "But I didn't transfer the data contained in the keys. Without the data, the Toreq Arch Council couldn't draw conclusions." He clasped his hands together. "Thus, making it impossible for them to decide whether or not to send their best military ships through the wormhole before it closed."

Ben blew air out of his puffed cheeks.

"Plus, I told them something you told me," Mesmo continued.

Ben tensed. "R-really?"

Mesmo nodded. "An Observer is not chosen at random. He or she is elected by the Arch Council after much debate and from a large pool of candidates. The one considered the most apt for the mission carries a lot of weight in the decision for, or against, the human race."

He paused. "You said you forgave your father because at least he had tried to make things right, even if he made bad choices."

Ben raised his eyebrow, trying to get his point.

"So, I, as the appointed Observer, recommended to the Toreq that they should apply the same thought to humans. Humans make bad choices sometimes, but at least they're trying."

Ben stared at the ground.

"Not to mention," Mesmo continued, "that you chose the life of a bee colony over your own..." he broke off, and his voice dropped. "That gives me hope."

Ben blushed and smiled shyly, considering his words as he drew a shape in the dirt with his shoe. How could humans ever come to understand the minds of the Toreq? If ever the A'hmun and the Toreq had once been like brothers, that time had long evaporated from human memory, lost in a blurry prehistory that came to state the human race originated on Earth.

"So, what's going to happen now?"

"Well, I finished analyzing the data contained in the seven keys. I will seek advice from the Wise Ones—some are favourable to the survival of your species, even if the data isn't. Then I will have to convince your leaders that they must act before it is too late. Humans will have to learn to change the way they live, to respect the land and other animal species and to create and nurture, instead of take, and destroy. Only then will the Toreq truly consider pardoning the descendants of the A'hmun." He paused, then added, "It's going to take many years of convincing and a lot of travelling. Two centuries is not as long as you might think."

Ben bit his lower lip and stared at his feet. "That sounds like an awful lot of work," he said.

"It is. But it can be done. I have to try."

Ben pouted and studied a particularly interesting blade of grass.

Mesmo nudged him.

The boy lifted his head and found the alien smiling at him.

"Will you help me?" Mesmo asked.

Ben broke into a grin. "I thought you'd never ask," he said.

EPILOGUE

Day turned into night. Shadows chased each other across the land. City lights came on, mirroring the stars. Coyotes scavenged for prey, hawks settled into their nests, and whales sank deep into the ocean.

The Earth drifted in space, oblivious to the sounds of laughter, conversations and bustling cities that dwelled on it.

Its faithful companion, the Moon, spread its white blanket over the sleeping souls, while beyond, all was silent.

The planets of the Solar System danced around their radiant king, as they had done for billions of years, and all was well in the Universe.

Or was it?

A low humming reverberated in a corner of space. Upon closer inspection, one could pinpoint the origin of the sound to a ghostly moon that belonged to the ringed planet, Saturn. Its unusual proximity to its massive ringed neighbour caused friction deep within its icy surface, resulting in giant geysers of water vapour being ejected into the vacuum of space, feeding Saturn's rings with its material.

It was somewhere in between these two celestial companions, in a blind spot from prying human eyes, that the friction was at its strongest, and water vapour from Enceladus swirled into a pinpoint of nothingness.

This hole, the size of a needle in terms of space measurements, collapsed in on itself, yet not before spewing out five dark spacecraft as it closed.

The impressive ships came to a complete standstill, only visible because their shapes hid the stars behind them.

Crackling sounds like static bounced between them, while sophisticated equipment would have caught the sound of low, metallic voices.

Within the largest spaceship, a tall man with white hair combed to the back and attached in a thin, waist-length braid surveyed the fleet. His small, honey-coloured eyes were hard and his cheekbones, pronounced.

Word spread that the suicidal wormhole crossing had been successfully completed in the nick of time.

But all in all, this event represented a mere ripple in the fabric of the cosmos.

THE ADVENTURE CONTINUES:
Ben Archer and the World Beyond
(The Alien Skill Series, Book 4)
https://www.amazon.com/dp/1989605044

LEAVE A REVIEW:
If you enjoyed this book, please leave a review in the 'Write a customer review' section:
https://www.amazon.com/dp/1989605141

PREQUEL:
Read the prequel to The Alien Skill Series,
The Great War of the Kins:
www.raeknightly.com

The Alien Skill Series continues!

Turn the page and start reading...

CHAPTER 1 *Motu Oné*

Ben Archer pressed his forehead against the window of the spaceship. The crystalline waters of French Polynesia stretched out before him. An uninhabited island curved out of the sea to his right, displaying its sugar-coated beaches, lush bushes and coconut palms.

The alien who sat at the controls by Ben's side brought the spacecraft to a gentle stop, letting it hover above the water without making a sound.

The size of a fighter jet with two sets of wings and just enough room to fit eight people in its hull, the black craft escaped radar detection with ease. Nevertheless, the thirteen-year-old squinted as he scanned the sparkling horizon, confirming that no humans sailed in the vicinity. Cumbersome reports of UFO sightings could complicate their mission and were best avoided at this point.

Ben puffed his cheeks, the hot cabin making him sweaty under his diving suit.

Guess the Toreq forgot to install air conditioning...

"Mesmo, are we going or what?" he said, backing away from the spacious window and throwing an annoyed look at the humanoid. "Gotta save the world, remember?"

The coral reefs off Motu Oné, one of a string of islands in the remote South Pacific Ocean, had been on Ben's mind for weeks. Yet, now that he was here, at last, Ben had to admit he had gotten up on the wrong side of the bed. Ever since he'd said goodbye to his mother that Sunday morning, a dark cloud had followed him from his pillow to this idyllic place. Mulling over why that could be, he picked up one of his fins and fought to pull the sticky rubber over his foot.

Mesmo didn't answer—too absorbed with his task as he shifted through holographic screens that floated before his face. The shadow of intricate symbols scrolled down the man's high cheekbones and honey-coloured eyes.

Irritated that the alien didn't answer, Ben sighed and crossed the hollow interior of the vessel to activate a switch. It released a metallic door that slid open, letting in a hot breeze that smelled of summer at the beach. He plopped down at the edge of the opening, swung his bare feet outside and dipped his toes into the transparent sea, admiring the pure white sand that lay ten feet below the surface. He reached for one of his fins and squeezed his eyes shut as he tried to pull it over his foot.

"Give me a moment," Mesmo said in a delayed response to Ben's question.

Ben knew he was reviewing the data given to him by one of the Wise Ones, who had last studied the area five years ago. "Jeez! You've gone over that ten times already," he said, grimacing as he struggled to put on the second fin. "Let's get our message out, Mesmo."

"You're right," Mesmo said, tearing his eyes away from the screens and leaning back in the pilot seat. He clapped his hands together. "Let's do this."

Ben watched him from the corner of his eye, becoming seriously offended with the uncooperative fin. "Mom's gonna need to dye your hair brown again," he said, noting that the roots of Mesmo's hair had turned white. Even though he looked like a normal man, the alien's otherwise bleach-white hair and unusual height could stick in people's minds.

"Yes, she told me." The alien tossed his flip-flops aside and removed his Hawaiian t-shirt, revealing his tanned torso. "So, are we going or what?" he poked, before taking three big strides across the egg-shaped interior and executing a perfect dive.

"Show off," Ben muttered, then whooped as his foot slipped into the stupid fin.

Mesmo resurfaced. He turned to face Ben and pointed behind him. "The coral reef's that way. Or we could try our luck farther out. There's a five thousand foot drop nearby—the entrance to the Pacific Ocean. Might be interesting..."

"No, thanks," Ben cut in, slipping his mask over his head and eyes. "I'm not trained for the deep yet. And besides, it would take me hours to decompress." He tapped his pressure gauge with his fingers.

"Come on, Benjamin, you don't need that old diving stuff. You know I can take both of us underwater." Mesmo's hands began to glow as he called up his inner power. The alien's fingers released a blue force that dented the surface of the sea until it reached Ben's feet. A large bubble surged from the water before the boy.

Trying to hide his admiration, Ben strapped the air tank to his back. "Jeez', Mesmo. We've been over this. You know I have to do this on my own. It's not like you're going to be around every time I need your water skill. And this *old diving stuff*—as you say—is the best my backward little civilization has got for now, so deal with it."

"Suit yourself." Mesmo shrugged with a smile. His hands stopped glowing, and the bubble burst, splashing Ben.

"Ha-ha." Ben grimaced, before shoving the snorkel in his mouth and placing his hands at the edge of the door. But his right hand slipped on the wet surface, sending him tumbling out of the spaceship. The side of his head hit the water, shoving liquid into his mask. He tore at it, sending stinging salt water up his nose in the process.

Spluttering and wiping at his face, Ben found Mesmo staring at him with one eyebrow raised. "Are you okay?"

Ben gagged at the sea-salt sliding down his throat. "Don't... you dare... laugh."

"I'm not," Mesmo said innocently, the corner of his mouth curling. "You know me. I'm incapable of humour."

"Yeah, right. But you sure learn fa..." Ben cut short because a familiar rushing sound filled his ears. He raised his hands, already expecting them to shine a clear blue. Ben closed his eyes and felt his own alien skill take over his human blood cells, the way it always did when an animal was nearby.

Trying to ignore his burning nose, Ben searched left and right. For the first time, he noticed how silent the ocean was. Wouldn't he be hearing a mingle of voices from sea creatures by now? He swam to the front of the spaceship and found the source that had activated his translation skill. A shiny black animal flopped around the surface. He reached out to it with his mind.

Hello? Are you in trouble?

Silence.

As he waded towards the creature through shallower water, Ben had to form a mental block to fend off fear that emanated from it.

Sh, it's okay. I'm here to help.

The animal twitched, and suddenly Ben recognized it.

A manta ray!

No bigger than a dinner plate, one of its triangular wings twisted in an awkward manner, deforming its sleek body. Leaning in closer, Ben understood the problem. The remains of a fishing net made from thin, nylon strings was wrapped around the young manta ray's body, pinning one of its wings over its back and hindering its movements.

Mesmo joined him, and they both set to work removing the entangled mesh. When they released the pectoral fin, the manta ray slid away in a hurry.

Ben and Mesmo exchanged a glance.

"It wouldn't even let me talk to it," Ben said, disappointed.

The alien placed a reassuring hand on his shoulder. "It's okay. We'll have better luck at the coral reef. They will listen to you there."

Ben tightened his grip on the nylon strings. "I hope so," he said. "Our lives depend on it."

Continue reading
Ben Archer and the World Beyond
(The Alien Skill Series, Book 4)
https://www.amazon.com/dp/1989605044

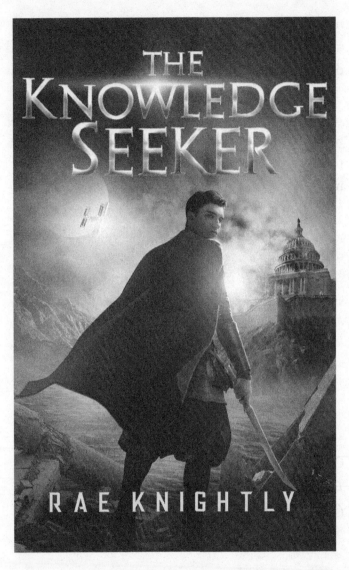

www.amazon.com/dp/1989605311

About the Author

Rae Knightly invites the young reader on a journey into the imagination, where science fiction and fantasy blend into the real world. Young heroes are taken on gripping adventures full of discovery and story twists.

Rae Knightly lives in Vancouver with her husband and two children. The breathtaking landscapes of British Columbia have inspired her to write The Alien Skill Series.

Follow Rae Knightly on social media:
Facebook/Instagram/Twitter/Pinterest
E-mail: raeknightly@gmail.com

Acknowledgments

To Cora, Jonathan and Bob for their valuable
insights.
To the people behind the scenes without whose
guidance this book would not be what it is.

To you, reader, for taking the time to read
Ben Archer and the Moon Paradox.
Thank you!
Rae Knightly